UNTAMED

M. O'Keefe

CHAPTER ONE

Poppy

THE IRISH NIGHT was thick velvet around the car. A darkness so dense and plush it felt like we were being swallowed whole.

In the back seat, Eden Morelli was quiet, a small miracle, so I guessed she was asleep. All her machinations to escape the death sentence waiting for her in the States had worked and she was bringing home the missing Morelli boy and his bride.

Glad it's working out for someone in this car.

Beside me, Ronan shifted gears, his focused gaze checking mirrors as he pushed the car faster through traffic. *My husband.* It didn't just seem strange. Strange would be a relief. Strange would be something I could laugh about.

"Isn't it wild?" I could say. "We're *married.*"

But being married to Ronan was something well past strange. It was terrifying. Infuriating. Exciting.

A pig truck was in the wrong lane and going too slow for Ronan. He passed on the shoulder and the loose gravel under the car's wheels made us fishtail. I braced myself against the dash. "Why do we have to go so fast?" I cried, my voice shaky with nerves, thick with emotion.

"The sooner we get back to New York, the sooner this is done."

And our marriage could be annulled. And he could do what he had planned to do since the moment he started playing with me like a dangerous cat with a stupid mouse. Leave me.

"Ronan," I whispered.

His eyes met mine in the dark. "What?"

Please. Please go back to who you were in the cottage. Please go back to smiling at me. Please give me something to hold on to so I'm not so scared. We were married. We were friends...sort of. Friendly?

He'd told me his secrets in the quiet of that cottage, revealing the wounds of his childhood. And I did the same. Though now, in the cold of this car, in the chill of his silence, it felt like all of that had happened to someone else. A different woman. A very different man. There was no softness in him now. And the secrets we'd traded were buried again.

"I want to see my sister," I said, instead of any

of that. I wanted to sound strong and impervious and as remote as Ronan—*my husband*—and I did. I sounded like a total bitch and I loved it. Small victories. "I need to see my sister."

"It's not safe."

"Nothing is anymore," I snarled, pushed to the very edge. "So what does it matter?"

For the first time maybe since I met him, I had the sense that when he looked at me, he was really seeing me. Not as a mouse he could play with until I broke. Not as a woman he could get to moan and beg. But a person he needed to reckon with. A person with power he could not take away. Or maybe I was exhausted and disoriented by the lights of the highway. Maybe I was only seeing what I wanted to see. Yeah, that sounded like me.

He handed me the burner phone he'd been using at the cottage and it clicked against the monstrosity that was my wedding ring. The Morelli ring, a dark sapphire surrounded by a starburst of diamonds, was heavy and too big. It looked beyond old-fashioned. Something more than a generational heirloom. It looked like a medieval museum piece, something used by ancient women to hold poison or bring on curses. It was ugly.

It suited our unholy union. "Call her," he said, pointing at the phone I held in my hand, caught up in my own thoughts.

"What can I tell her?" I asked. "We will meet her at your apartment in London?"

"We're flying out tonight. To New York."

"Ronan," I gasped, my façade crumbling. "I need to see my sister. Please—"

He closed his eyes for a second like he was just so done with me. Fine. Good. I was done with him. How preposterous that it took marriage to get us here. To build the wall between us so high there was no getting over it. I called the last number dialed and my sister answered. "Poppy?" Zilla asked. "Where are you? Are you close?"

The plan—before Eden found us and opened up the Morelli vault of secrets and changed the course of our lives—had been for me to go to London to get to my sister while Ronan went back to New York and found out why the Morelli's wanted me dead or alive. "I'm…" I turned my back to Ronan as best I could in the small car, fighting for a tiny bit of privacy no matter how ridiculous. "I can't come, Zilla."

"What do you mean you can't come? You're on your way."

I swallowed. "Our plans changed."

"Are you in trouble? Are you safe?" Safe? That was painfully relative, wasn't it? I was in a car, I was married to a killer. A killer who swore to protect me. To worship my body with his. *But we're ignoring that part.* "I'm fine," I whispered. "But I can't come to you right now. I'm going back to New York."

"Then I'll come back to New York, too."

"I don't know…" I turned to look at Ronan, only to find him watching me. "Is it safe for her to go back to New York?"

"My man Jacob is there," Eden said from the back seat. "He can come back with her. He makes every place safe."

"He's there? Where?" Ronan asked, looking at Eden in the rearview mirror.

"London. Your safe house is not the secret you thought it was. He wanted to watch her," Eden said, and I could hear her shrug. "I figured it wasn't a bad idea. You guys leave leverage that can be used against you everywhere you go."

Ronan turned his head to look at me. And for a moment his face revealed his emotions. Volatile and dark. And in the lack of real warmth between us, those feelings felt white hot. And as much as I wanted to reach out my fingers and warm myself against him, I knew it was false.

He seemed warm because I was so, so cold.

He turned his eyes back on the road. "I'll have arrangements made for them to get back to the States."

"Instructions will come to you for how you can get back to the city," I said into the phone. "Eden Morelli left a man looking after you at the London apartment," I said. "He'll come back with you. He looks—"

"Like a goddamn accountant," my sister said.

"He's not. He's absolutely not."

"No shit," Zilla said. "When I get back to Bishop's Landing, I'll come to your house. I gotta warn you, it's pretty trashed, but we can fix it back up."

I closed my eyes, thought of that stupid shower I'd built. That backyard I'd tried to turn into something I could call my own. And none of it mattered. It wasn't a home. It was just a place.

"It's not my house anymore," I said. "It's not safe."

"Then you can get to my apartment. I'll take care of you for once."

Until we figured out what everyone wanted from us, my only safe place was beside Ronan. The ties that bound us together were varied and never-ending.

"I'm staying with Ronan."

"Ronan Byrne? The fucking kidnapper? The killer?"

Husband.

But I kept that to myself.

"Poppy? What are you doing?" she whispered into my silence.

The answer, like it had been through most of my life, was simple. "I'm doing what I have to to survive," I told my sister, with more edge than I should. "I'll be in touch when we're in New York. Be safe, Zilla. I love you."

"Oh, Poppy. I love you too and please, please be careful with Ronan. You can't trust him."

Like I didn't know that. Ronan would keep my body safe and incinerate my heart. Trusting him would be my worst mistake.

"I'll be okay," I said. I waited until Zilla hung up and then I pressed the phone to my lips and closed my burning eyes, missing my sister but unable to feel it with the ache of everything else in my body.

"Poppy?" Ronan asked, and with my back still to him, unwilling to show him anything else when I'd already shown him so much, I tossed his phone at him over my shoulder. I heard it thunk against the dashboard. Being childish felt good.

And I was never childish. It had always seemed selfish to rail against the things I couldn't control. But right now? Oh…I felt a real temper tantrum coming on.

"We'll be at the airport in an hour," he said in a quiet voice. What was there to say to that? What was there even to feel about it? I kept my mouth shut and tried not to cry.

"Here." From between my seat and the door appeared Eden's hand and a pretty silver flask. "You need it more than I do."

I grabbed on to that flask like it would keep me from drowning. And I drank.

CHAPTER TWO

THE JET WAS sleek and modern. The smiling attendant checked us in, got us settled. She wore a black pencil skirt and a black button-down shirt and she looked somehow sexy and professional at the same time.

"Mr. Byrne," she said to Ronan, her voice pitched low. "Welcome aboard."

He paid her little to no attention and still I managed to be jealous. Which wasn't fun. Or reasonable. "I would like a drink," I said to her.

"Of course." She smiled at me. "What kind?"

"One with booze."

"Champagne," Eden said. She sat next to me on the long banquet seating, the white leather smooth and expensive beneath my legs. "We'll have a bottle of champagne."

Ronan walked through a doorway into a back bedroom. Despite the ambient noise of the jet, I heard a shower turn on. At some point in the day—between breakfast and getting married—he'd been sprayed with blood. It somehow worked during our savage ceremony, but now that we were heading back to civilization, that madman who'd told me he'd worship my body with his had to be put away. Replaced by that stone-faced killer he'd been before. If it weren't for the bloodstained cloth in my back pocket and the giant ugly ring on my finger, it could have been a nightmare.

Our champagne was delivered, popped and poured and before I could register even taking off—it seemed we were in the air. I spun the ring on my finger and drowned my sorrows in expensive bubbly.

It wasn't all that different from the night I met Ronan. The engagement ring on my finger had been another man's. And the champagne had been Caroline's. *I really needed to start buying my own jewelry and my own fucking champagne.*

But the rage was all mine.

"What are you going to do?" Eden asked. "When you get back?" She was like a jaguar trying to make polite conversation. She wore her fur coat; the black dress beneath it poured over every curve. She'd reapplied her red lipstick and pulled all that black hair up into a messy bun on the top of her head. A jaguar at the end of a long day.

Admittedly, I was a little drunk and my world

was utter chaos, but I remembered with sudden and exciting clarity how she'd hit on me. Twice.

My marriage to Ronan seemed to have changed dramatically the way he talked to me. Looked at me. It was nice to think that someone on this plane might still find me…desirable. It was a weird, selfish comfort but whatever. This was a cold dark night and I was taking what I could.

Taking what I could. There was Ronan in the cottage, telling me that as he crouched over my naked body. *There is only what you take.*

How clearly I understood that now. I'd waited my whole life for people to give me things. Crumbs of affection. Opportunities. A way to keep me and my sister safe. That was over. I would take what I needed. What I wanted. I drained my champagne flute and held out my glass for more. Eden obliged. "I'm not thinking about tomorrow," I said.

"Probably smart," Eden agreed. We both sipped our champagne, the hum of the engines quieter than on a big commercial jet. Almost like a purr. "For what it's worth?" she said. "I'm sorry."

"Sorry?" I almost spat the word. God, how much of my life had I spent apologizing. Sorry for who I was and who my sister was and what our parents had done to us. I looked at Eden, the sexy jaguar in the sexy jaguar dress. "Stop being sorry. It doesn't change anything."

She blinked at me and I looked away, enraged by her surprise. *Even a mouse gets pissed if you fuck up her life enough times.* The back door to the jet's cabin opened and Ronan was there, wearing dark slacks and a darker sweater. Clothes that were on this jet, apparently. His jet. Evidence was mounting that my husband was a very wealthy man.

There had been a meeting with lawyers before my marriage to the senator. A prenup we'd signed basically stipulated that if I left him for any reason, I got nothing. I'd signed it because I had nothing to begin with. And, of course, because I was dumb.

Maybe when Ronan was done with me, I'd take all his money. Especially this jet with its leather and champagne. His hair was damp and he'd shaved. The dark growth of his beard was gone, removing all resemblance to the softer man at the cabin. I would mourn the loss of that guy maybe for the rest of my life.

Now his face was back to unforgiving lines and narrowed eyes and a mouth I wanted to kiss until it was familiar.

I took a sip of my champagne that ended up being half the glass and held it out for Eden to refill. She made some scoffing noise in her throat but filled my glass.

That's right, I thought, getting into the spirit of things.

He sat down opposite me on another long banquette. Our attendant arrived and asked him in a low voice if he wanted anything. Ronan's clear crisp eyes took in our half bottle of champagne and our glasses and he shook his head. Like someone on this plane needed to keep their wits about them. The attendant vanished again, leaving us alone with the hum of the motor and the threat of what would happen when we arrived back in New York.

It occurred to me, suddenly, that one of us— or all of us—could die. It wasn't such a leap to make. Ronan and Eden's hired killer had left a trail of bodies in Carrickfergus. I had, up until my marriage, been wanted dead or alive. And just about everyone who knew Ronan probably wanted to kill him at some point. I was trying not to be dramatic, but it really seemed like all signs were pointing to more bloodshed.

"I talked to Niamh," Ronan said. "She found

the bankers box at your house."

"Really?" That seemed like an impossible long shot.

"She'll deliver it to our apartment tomorrow."

"Our?"

He glanced at me and then away and I liked it. I liked how for once in my life I was controlling the temperature in the room. It was…exciting. And perhaps it was the champagne or the danger. But that excitement pooled between my legs and began to hum. Filling me with reckless energy.

More champagne.

"What answers do you think we're going to find in that bankers box?" I asked, crossing my legs like I was wearing a formal gown from my previous life and not a pair of black jeans and a borrowed flannel shirt and still no goddamned underwear.

"Why Caroline wanted you to marry the senator. What he was doing for the Morellis and why they wanted you dead or alive."

"That's a lot of work for a bankers box," I said.

"I don't know who the hell you've turned into," Eden laughed, "but I like her. I like her a lot."

"You liked the old me enough to want to fuck me," I said, reckless and dangerous, and again the temperature in the cabin changed. The energy coiled and it was like each of us took a deep breath and held it.

"You should get some sleep." Ronan's voice was quiet and firm and I remembered the girl on that side lawn, the first time he used that voice. The way I'd wanted to do what he said. The way I craved his attention and approval.

"It's my wedding night," I said. I met his beautiful blue gaze and didn't look away. My entire body shuddered with a memory, physical and real as if it were happening now and here rather than days ago. His body over mine, the thick head of his cock just inside of me. Just enough to hurt and feel better than anything ever had before in my life.

For that shaking and delicious second, I'd had the power. And he'd been helpless against me.

Yeah. I'll have a side of *that* feeling with my champagne.

"It's your wedding night, too," I said, which was somehow the weapon that made him look away. His eyes on the dark sky out the window. His jaw tight. "Someone should get fucked."

In the stone-cold silence, I drained the last of

my champagne.

"Is this…a volunteer situation?" Eden asked, looking between Ronan and me.

"You're drunk," Ronan said, as scathing as he could be, which was pretty damn awful. I wasn't drunk. Adrenaline was eating up the alcohol as fast as I could drink it. But I was in that dangerous place, that shaded gray between completely in and completely out of control. *Maybe*, I thought. *Maybe this is where I'll be from now on.* I stood up, my legs spread wide so I didn't topple in the slight movement of the plane. Eden was looking at me like a prize she'd won. Like we were in a cartoon and she was starving in the desert and I'd turned into a big chicken leg.

Stand up, I thought at her.

Like she heard me, like I was super powerful, she did, her body small and curvy and two inches from mine. The plane shimmied in turbulence and that was all it took for her body to brush mine. Our breasts. Our bellies. She reached out a hand to steady herself and I grabbed it with mine. *I'm using you,* I thought. I*'m using you to make him do something. To provoke him into action.* But then, she'd used us to save her own damn life, so maybe things were even.

"How sorry are you for making us get married

and bringing us back here?" I asked her.

Her eyes ignited. "Very very sorry."

"Have you ever kissed a woman?" Ronan asked, pulling my attention back to him. He sat, a dark shadow on all that cream leather. His leg was crossed, an ankle on his knee, and his arm was stretched out along the back of the banquette. He looked casual. Uninterested.

"Yes," I said, surprising both of them. College. A party gone a little wild. A blonde volleyball player had kissed me and I had kissed her back until some frat boy came in and snapped a picture. The volleyball player had punched the frat boy in the face and deleted the picture off his phone. I'd spent the next week grappling with my sexuality and identity, and the next time I saw the volleyball player she'd moved on to the arms of a woman who worked in the student union.

"Did you like it?" Eden asked. There was a chance I had liked the idea of it more than the actual kiss, preoccupied as I'd been by the fact that I was kissing a woman.

"I don't remember," I said.

Eden smiled. She really was so pretty with all her manipulations and bright red lips. "Let's try and jog your memory."

The hand I wasn't holding slipped up to cup

my face. She wore heels and I wore boots that weren't mine. But the heels gave her enough height that I didn't have to bend and she didn't have to stand on tiptoe. Our lips met carefully and softly, sweetly almost, and it was a surprise. I was using her to make my reluctant husband jealous and she'd leveraged my entire future to keep herself alive. Gentleness would have been the last thing I expected. And, truthfully, I didn't think I wanted it. I wanted rough and wild and nearly violent. I wanted to use and be used.

I wanted power and control and for someone, one of us, any of us, to feel *something*. The gentleness reminded me that I was human. That she was human. That our bodies were fragile and the night had had terrible trauma.

I gasped, my lips opening against hers.

"Shhh," she whispered like she knew exactly what I was thinking. She stepped closer, pulling my body against hers. Her hand against my cheek slid to my neck and held me there. Our kiss went from tentative—from a show I was putting on for my dispassionate husband—to something I needed. Connection in a world that had been turned upside down.

I dropped her hand and grabbed her hips, pulling her to me. Holding her tight and close.

Kissing her with more passion than I thought I felt. But the hum that had settled between my legs had exploded in my body. And I wanted Eden. I wanted Ronan. I wanted *everything.* I broke the kiss and turned to look at him. Eden kissed her way down my neck, pulling open my flannel shirt one button at a time. My lips were swollen and my eyes were heavy.

She licked the top of my breast and I groaned, never looking away from his eyes.

I wore no bra, and when Eden opened my shirt enough, she pulled my nipple into her mouth. My head fell back and my eyes wanted to close but I didn't let them. I watched him, watching us. The way his eyes went from cold and distant to fiery. To intense.

He shifted, uncrossing his legs and stretching them out wide, and I knew he was getting hard. Watching us. Eden's hands cupped my breasts, her thumbs stroking my nipples.

"Ronan," I breathed. Eden turned to face him and I couldn't see us, but I could see his reaction to us. He was not unmoved. But he didn't get up. He only watched. The disappointment I felt was so sharp. So keen it took me a second to get my breath.

I craved him. Needed him. The only way any

of this made sense was if he was touching me. If he was wanting me like I wanted him. But he did not move. He did not say a word and I wondered, suddenly, if this was the only way left for me to have him. He wouldn't touch me. But he would watch someone else do it.

"She's beautiful," Eden said.

"She is," he said, his dark voice filling the cabin, and my knees went loose.

"So soft. Fragile." Eden's hands spanned my waist, her fingers edging towards the buttons of my pants.

"She's tougher than she looks," Ronan said, and it was as close to a compliment as I'd heard from him.

"She kisses like a virgin," Eden said and I scowled.

"She practically is," Ronan said. "She should be."

"Should we pretend she is?" Eden asked, walking around my body, turning me to face him. She cupped my breasts, teased my nipples with feather-light touches that made me crazy. I whimpered in my throat. "A virgin on her wedding night, sacrificed to two terrible people who shouldn't be touching her soft, sacred body?"

"No," I said. I didn't want to pretend that. I

was done being sacred.

"Good. Virginity is overrated," Eden said, like an expert. Her fingers on my nipples were suddenly rough.

"Fuck," I breathed, resting my head against her shoulder, everything spinning in the best possible way.

"Tell me what she likes," Eden asked him as she touched me. "Tell me how to touch her. Make it good for her. For her wedding night."

Ronan was silent. And my body still hummed and I was strangely grateful to Eden for the way it seemed she had read my mind. The way she'd tried to pull him in because she knew that was what I needed. But he wasn't playing along, which honestly, I should have known. My eyes closed, blocking him out, because this connection through Eden didn't feel like enough. This connection felt like loss. "Over her jeans," he said, his voice like gravel, and I gasped from the relief. "Touch her through her jeans. She likes it hard. A little rough."

I kept my eyes closed as my heart pounded in my throat. Eden skipped the button and the zipper and instead she slid her fingers right along the seam, pushing them hard against me until I gasped. Until my knees really did buckle. "Wait,"

I breathed, grabbing on to her wrist.

"No," he said. "Don't let her catch her breath. This was what she wanted."

"What do you want?" Eden asked in my ear, still giving me the power that Ronan was trying to take away from me.

"She wants to come," Ronan answered for me. "Don't you, Poppy? You want her to make you come. To put her fingers inside of you. You want her to bite on your nipple just the way you like and whisper something dirty in your ear. Something about what a good girl you are and how pretty your tits are and how she's going to use you so hard, until it doesn't hurt to think about what's going to happen next."

"Yes," I sobbed. Eden's hands left me and my eyes opened wide, hoping it was because Ronan would be there, giving me what I needed. But no, Eden just pushed me back so I was sitting on the banquette again, legs splayed, breasts bared. I had to look wild. Feral. My eyes met Ronan's and still he sat there. If he hadn't just said those words, I would have thought he wasn't even paying attention. He was so calm. So…unbothered. I undid my pants myself, shoved them down my thighs, revealing my body.

"Don't." He stopped. Looked away. Again,

the hard clench of his jaw. He cared about something. But what? He didn't want to see me naked? Or he didn't want any of this?

Jesus, Poppy. He'd done nothing but make that clear.

I'd stepped into waters so deep and so turbulent I was drowning. I crossed my arms over my body, feeling as if I would explode from want and embarrassment.

"Oh no, sweetheart," Eden said, quietly, like she was talking just to me. "That's not what he wants."

"I don't know what he wants," I whispered. "I've never known what he wants."

Eden pulled up her skirt high over her own hips, revealing a black satin thong, wet between her legs, pulled askew. I reached up and touched her, ran my thumb along the fat seam between the lips of her pussy. She was so wet. Swollen and hot. My body kept humming and she bit her lip.

"Honey," she whispered. "He's not interested in watching me come. He wants to watch you come. So let's...let's give him that."

"Why are you doing this?" I whispered.

"Because I fucked up your lives pretty good," she said. "I owe you. And this is a goddamned delightful debt to pay. They should all be so fucking hot." She pushed me forward until I was on the edge of the seat and then she pulled me back against her chest, so I was reclining in her arms. Across from us, Ronan was looking out the window, his cheeks flushed, his jaw tight but his eyes very carefully, very deliberately, not on us. Eden's hands cupped my breasts, lifting them like she was offering them to him.

Still he didn't look.

She pinched my nipples and he was utterly indifferent. We might as well have been reading the paper. He wasn't going to break. Everything I was doing, all the ways I was trying to provoke him and he didn't care. Ronan never cared. A sound came out of me, a sobbing moan from the very place in my chest where my heart was being twisted and broken.

That sound made him turn his head. Our eyes met in the burning distance between us and I saw everything that had happened between us. The engagement party, my kitchen, the gala, Caroline's house, Ireland…all of it. Every moment of Ronan and Poppy was in his eyes. Eden touched my knee, pushing my leg out wide.

"Now," Eden purred. "When you say rough, how rough?" Her fingers slid from my knee to my pussy and I arched into her. This build-up had been days in the making and I was suddenly desperate. Burning. An orgasm building in my clit. A small touch. A tiny bit of pressure and I would explode into a million pieces.

"Stop," he demanded. Barked, really. Eden stopped, her fingers on my belly. But I was too far gone. My hips arched, my own hands reaching between my legs to give me the relief I needed. I was past wanting to feel good. Wanting a wedding night. I was in some kind of animal need. Desperate.

"Stop her," he growled, and Eden grabbed my hands, pulling them away.

"What…what are you doing?" I whispered, my body arcing up and away from Eden's towards him. Needing…him.

"I think you've awakened the beast," Eden purred, her fingers like manacles around my wrist. "And I think the beast doesn't want anyone touching you but him."

I started to close my legs. "Ah ah ah," she said and used our linked hands to keep my legs wide. Open. For him. I liked this too much. The orgasm built despite not being touched. *Because* I wasn't being touched.

"Is that true?" I asked him.

He said nothing, his jaw moving like his teeth

needed to be punished. Oh fuck. I lifted my hips again. *Punished.* I wanted to be punished. "You don't want anyone touching me but you?" Eden wasn't very strong and she certainly wasn't trying too hard to restrain me. I think she was on my side more than his when it came to this little power struggle, so when I pulled my hand back between my legs, she didn't try too hard to stop me. In fact, when I switched my grip so it was my hand holding hers and I pushed her fingers down on my clit, she did it with some eagerness.

"Fuck," she groaned and bit my shoulder. "You are the hottest goddamn thing."

"You don't want her to touch me because I'm your wife?" I asked, pushing Eden's fingers against me just the way I liked. The way he taught me to like. My eyes never leaving his face. "I'm going to come," I said. "And if you won't—"

"No." He stood and Eden flinched, and even I felt a moment of hesitation. A real and cold fear of him. He walked over to us and leaned down, just a little. Enough to put one hand against my chest, his fingers curling around my neck. His other hand knocked Eden's fingers away so his palm cupped me. Long and thick, his fingers slid down between the thick, wet and hot folds between my legs to tease the entrance of my body.

I gasped and shook and pushed myself against him. He held me down, against Eden.

"This is mine," he said. His fingers speared inside of me and I screamed at the pleasure/pain of it. "No one touches this but me."

The orgasm was coming. So hard and so fierce I was shaking. I could actually feel tears burning in my eyes. Eden's hands were cupping my breasts, teasing my nipples, and he must not have minded that because his eyes burned as he watched. I was held open for him. Pried open by him. "You can play all the fucking games you want, Poppy but this…this is mine."

"Then take it," I said.

We were all frozen in the moment. Stay or go. Love me or deny me.

I'd gambled everything on this one thing and I had no idea what he would do. His hands left my body and without them I felt like I might float away on the pain. On the ache of wanting so much from him and always being denied.

But then he scooped me up in his arms, cradling me against his chest. I wrapped my arms around his neck, buried my face against his chest, breathing him in. From the floor he grabbed my pants and carried me away from Eden to the back cabin. To a place where it was quiet and dark and just us.

He slammed shut the door behind him, like he could stop time. Like he could stop this plane's travel through the sky back to the city and the people who would kill us. He tossed me on the bed where I bounced and spread my arms out wide so I didn't fall off.

"You're my wife," he said, saying the word like he was tasting every edge of it. He shook out my pants and found in the back pocket the bloody stretch of fabric that had tied our hands together during our ceremony.

"What are you going to do about it?" I asked, taunting him mercilessly.

CHAPTER THREE

Poppy

H E REACHED BEHIND his head and pulled off his fine, expensive sweater. His wiry strength was revealed, his sleek muscles across his chest, down to the waist of his pants. He was beautiful and sharp and I wanted him so much it hurt.

My eyes on his beautiful body, I lay back, my hand between my legs.

"Don't," he said.

"Or what?"

He grabbed my hand in a grip that was too rough, which made it perfect, and then he put one knee on the bed, making the mattress dip under his weight and my body rolled into his. He pushed my hand up over my head and then grabbed my other hand and forced it over my head too. With the bloody cloth that bound us in holy matrimony, he tied my hands together, the fabric rough against the tender skin of my wrists. I sucked in a breath. And then another.

He was silent, his eyes blazing over my body.

"Ronan," I whispered and reached for him with my bound hands, but he caught them and pressed them back to the bed over my head. He slid the palm of his other hand between my legs and gave me that pressure I loved so much against my clit. And I could have nodded. I could have said yes. I wanted to. Lord knows at the moment I would have said yes to anything. But we'd done all of this before, this territory of his hand between my legs and me coming alone while he held himself aloof was well traveled and I couldn't do it again.

There was something I wanted. Something he'd been keeping from me all this time and his reasons were noble and very nearly kind. But we were past nobility and kindness. If I was his, then he was mine.

"Only if you fuck me. *Husband*." The word was an endearment and a curse. I wanted him and I was scared of him.

I could love him if he'd let me and he would undoubtedly destroy me. "You're my husband." Whatever control he'd been clinging to snapped in his hands and he fell onto my body, his mouth finding my breast, pulling a nipple into his mouth as he undid his pants, cupped his cock, stroking the length, holding the tip as come oozed out. I wanted to lean down, put him in my mouth. I wanted to taste him. I wanted to be covered in him and by him. I wanted to soak him into my skin and hide him behind my heart.

"I've got no fucking condom," he said in his thick accent, his old code standing strong even under this onslaught.

"I'm your wife," I said. The word mapped the unknown and treacherous space between us. *Wife.* It was my key into all the places he kept dark and secret. If he would only let me in. I met his eyes and for a second it was as if Eden and the plane and the danger that waited for us was gone. And it was just us. Ronan and Poppy so deeply mad for each other, so painfully entwined that whatever happened after this didn't matter. Couldn't possibly matter.

If I got pregnant, then it was meant to be.

That's how it felt right now. Like the stars had aligned and I saw the same leap of faith in his eyes. Or maybe it was just the sight of me, wet and pink and *his*.

"You can't go back, *a chuisle*." The words were practically lost in his thick accent. And then he took my bound hands in his and braced them over my head, and with his other he guided his cock to the entrance of my body. And I was wet and I was ready but he was so big. Between my legs I stretched and burned and I pushed my head back against the mattress. Tears trickled out of my eyes.

"Shhh," he whispered, stroking my neck, my breasts. "You can take it. You can take it all. Look." He touched my chin and I looked down, the sight of Ronan's thick cock splitting me open. "Look at how hot you are. How fucking perfect you are. Such a good girl. Taking my cock. Such a good fucking girl."

His words became gibberish in my ear as the pain became pleasure and then back again.

"I can't—" I whimpered. Ronan's eyes met mine, wild and dark, and I saw in the killer the boy he'd been. Unsure and scared and he would pull out and leave me, that's how badly he didn't want me to be hurt. But then he'd be gone for good. I would never get him back.

"Don't stop," I breathed. He shook his head. Sweat dripped from his hair and down his face and I reached for him with my bound hands, but he held me immobile, so I lifted my face to his, holding myself close so I could kiss him. Taste him. Breathe him in. He turned his face aside.

Like he didn't want to kiss me. But then he was inside of me and it was all I could do to keep breathing.

"You're my wife," he said. "Mine."

I arched against him, fucking myself on his cock, trying to somehow get closer. How ridiculous was that? He was as close as he'd ever been to me and it felt like he was miles away somehow. Was it Eden?

Was it because I'd forced this issue?

Was it, in the end, that none of this was anything he wanted? "Ronan," I breathed, wanting to tell him I was sorry. But I wasn't. I wasn't sorry at all. I would do it all again to be right here. He put his thumb against my clit and that was all it took. The pain was gone, the orgasm was back, and he was fucking me. Hard thrusts that pushed me back against the bed. We were sweat and skin and moans and gasps and I was coming. I was coming again. And Ronan kept fucking me like he had no intention of stopping, like he could do it forever.

"Ronan," I breathed. "Ronan. Come. Please. Come."

I could not come again. I could only slip my bound hands over his head and try as hard as I could not to count my mistakes while they were still happening. I could only try to hold on to my heart, forcing it to stay inside me and not go winging off to settle itself on him. I opened up my body and I opened up my soul and I prayed with everything in me that there would be something of me at the end of this. Some part of myself I hadn't given him.

"It's okay," I breathed into his ear. "You can let yourself go. It's okay. It's safe."

It was the opposite of safe, but I knew what was holding him back. Finally, he pushed his arms under my body, holding me as tight as he could as he shook and roared in my ear, thrusting into me so hard and so high it was like I could feel him in the back of my throat. He shook in my arms, almost like he was crying. The muscles of his back twitching. His face, sweaty and damp against mine, and I held him tight. Hard. Memorizing every single detail because I knew it would be a fight to get him back in my arms.

"Poppy," he breathed, trying to lift himself away from me.

"Stay," I said, holding him as hard as I could, but in the end my strength was nothing compared to his. My love was nothing compared to his will. He ducked out from under my bound arms and rolled off of me, letting me go, and the cold air of the cabin was freezing on my wet and bruised body. I shook once, like a flinch, and he made a noise in his throat, finding the edge of a blanket on the foot of the bed and covering me with it. His fingers traced the edge of the fabric that bound my hands. He touched the splatters of blood one by one.

Something about finally having sex with him felt...violent. We'd changed everything between us, and change that profound only came by way of brutality. Finally, he pulled the knot loose and unbound me, the fabric tossed onto the floor. I immediately felt the lack, my wrists colder than the rest of my body.

"Are you all right?" he asked, quietly.

"Fine," I croaked, my voice ruined. "You?"

He laughed once low in his throat and I looked at his profile, so sharp in the dark. *You were inside me. You came inside me. I might at this very moment be pregnant.* Almost unconsciously I tipped my hips, curled my knees up like I could hold his sperm inside of me. He looked over at me like he knew what I was doing.

A baby. We might have made a baby when we were hardly a couple. What kind of disaster was this? *He will not love me.* I knew that. He would never allow himself to love me and so I had to stop myself, right now, from loving him.

"That won't happen again," he said. "It can't."

I wrapped the blanket around me, shifting to stand up despite the sting and ache in my body. Between my legs I was wet and sore and I needed a shower. And a good long cry. I needed my sister and a change of clothes and some goddamned underwear.

"Poppy," he murmured.

"I'm going to take a shower."

"Are you all right?"

I turned and looked at him, my heart straining out of my grip. He was so beautiful. So tortured and still. "Why wouldn't I be?" I asked. "I'm your wife."

CHAPTER FOUR

Ronan

THE FIRST MAN I killed, I only knew his name. David Allen. And I knew he owed the wrong people—in this case, my boss—money. And there were rumors he'd been talking to the PSNI to get out of some trouble. And rumors like that were a death sentence. Enter me. I was seventeen years old and the gun I'd been handed by Ronald McMurphy was huge in my hand. A cartoon gun, like.

And I'd felt like a right proper mobster.

Like a terrible cliché, I broke into David Allen's kitchen in the dead of the night.

But climbing the stairs past all those pictures of his parents and the wife who'd just left him, I thought about my da's head bent in the rain and how the fireplace in our old house smelled like cedar and wet socks. And I had to pee so bad I thought I wouldn't be able to control it.

That I'd put a bullet in David Allen's head

and one in his hand (a little calling card from my boss as warning to any other scumbag thinking of talking to the PSNI—something about the hand that feeds you) and I'd piss myself.

Ronald would fucking kill himself laughing if I came back with that gun and smelling of piss.

David Allen had heard me on the steps and he'd woken up. When I came in he had the lamp on and he was reaching for something on his bedside table and I was sure it was a gun and so I didn't give him the tough-guy speech I'd had all worked up in my head. I just put a bullet in him. Cold as ice. And I thought I was *something.* Killing this man. Doing the job.

Wasn't I something?

When I stepped forward to put the bullet through his hand, I saw that he'd been reaching for a pair of glasses on the nightstand and I ran to the bathroom to throw up. That night I went home to my shitty apartment with all the locks and I did something I'd never done before. I prayed. I prayed for someone to come at that moment and do the same thing to me that I'd done to David Allen.

The regret that night was like the stones the priests put under our knees during mass at St. Brigid's. And I promised never again. I wouldn't be a killer.

There was wrong and then there was *wrong,* and my da was never proud of me, but now I was some kind of monster.

Ronald came over with a bottle of the good stuff and he ignored the tears on my face and the puke on my collar and told me it would get better. The regrets didn't last forever and after a few more jobs I'd have callouses built up so I didn't feel a thing, like.

And then he handed me an envelope with a thousand pounds in it.

More money than I'd ever seen in one place. The kind of money that changed a stupid fucking kid's life. And so I built up callouses. I did the job, I made the money and I moved on, allowing myself only one thing: the comfort that the men I killed were monsters. And you needed a monster to put down monsters. There was a logic to that and, I can admit it, a nobility to it that I liked. That allowed me to sleep at night.

Sort of.

But Poppy...sweet, innocent, reckless Poppy...my wife. *My wife.* I regretted her. From the second I met her and understood her fate.

From the moment I realized how Caroline used her and would keep using her.

I regretted tonight.

Even as I was getting hard again at the memory of her laid open for me in Eden's arms. Even as I thought about how she felt around my cock and wanted with every single breath in my body to get back inside of her, I *regretted* having been inside of her.

She had some perception that I was a good man. Worth saving. Worth *loving*.

Daft fucking princess.

All I have ever wanted, since she stepped out into that side yard, was to keep her safe. To keep her away from the worst of Caroline. The Morellis. Me. And now we were married.

She was in the shower and it was impossible not to imagine her body under the hot spray. Impossible not to imagine how I could go in there, strip off my clothes and climb into the shower with her. And she would fight.

Fuck, I hoped she would fight.

She might smack me and shove me. Call me something vicious and true and I would pin her back against the tiled shower and put my hand between her legs and find her wet and swollen and so fucking ready for me I could make her come just by saying her name.

I stood and pulled on my clothes, disgusted

with myself.

She might be pregnant. Right now. A baby. The shame was nearly as profound as my pleasure.

Not so high and mighty now, are ya, eejit? My father's voice could be counted on to keep track of my mistakes as I made them. I stood still in the quiet of the cabin, the hum of the engines all around me, listening for Poppy.

To hear if she was crying. Another wedding night for her that ended in tears. My plan had been to get her out of this marriage clean. And six hours in I'd already fucked her and possibly gotten her pregnant. When it came to Poppy, I was miles past regret. She was a whole different kind of torture.

In the cabin Poppy's clothes were folded and stacked on the edge of the banquette and Eden looked put back together. Red lipstick, tight black dress, fur coat, and a glass of champagne in her long-fingered hand—all of it armor. I met her eyes, and if Poppy were here, she would apologize for the way we left her, but I was not a man for apologies. She made her bed and she could manage herself just fine. "Is she okay?" she asked.

I laughed and poured myself a scotch, resisting the urge to drink it straight from the bottle where it was clipped in the bar. "Something about your concern doesn't feel genuine, Eden."

"She's a sweet girl," Eden said, and I found myself shaking my head. She had been a sweet girl. Years ago. Now…she was something else. Too reckless to be sweet. Too angry. She was dangerous. And I'd liked that sweet Poppy. The malleable Poppy, with her wide, blinking eyes and her shit self-esteem. I'd liked the way she looked at me out of the corner of her eye, the way she weighed a situation before deciding what to do or how to act.

But this woman? Who charged in blazing, demanding her due and fuck anyone in her way?

I would die for her.

And she could never fucking know or she would tie herself to me as I sank to the bottom of the world.

"Bryant received the photographs I sent him," Eden said, tapping on her phone.

"He's calling off his dogs?"

"For the moment."

"You going to crawl back to the Morellis with your tail between your legs?" I asked her, finishing what was left of Poppy's champagne.

"It's not that bad," Eden said, and I laughed. All her power was gone. All her leverage. All she had left was her life and she needed to figure that out quick. She was fucked and she knew it. She swallowed and glanced out the window at the dark night. "Will there be twenty Morellis waiting for me?"

"You're asking me if I called them?"

"Payback, maybe. For making you do this."

"I'm not interested in Poppy watching you get gunned down in front of her."

"Well, if that isn't a love song, I don't know what is."

"No one knows we're coming in," I said. "Not Caroline. Not the Morellis. You'll have time to plot your escape."

"Or my revenge," she said, attempting to be coy and cheeky.

"The best thing you can do is get the fuck out of town, Eden, before they even know you're here."

She shook her head at me. "You're so sure all the time, Ronan. One of these days you're going to be wrong."

It was, in fact, only a matter of fucking time. I'd spent the last ten years of my life waiting for the bullet in the back of my skull and I'd grown numb to fear or even anticipation. But now…with Poppy, the clock counting down the minutes I had left in my life was loud in my head.

"You're wrong about Poppy," she said.

"What the fuck do you know about it?"

"She thinks you're mad at her and you can punish her with your silences and broody Irish grunts. But I see the truth." She grinned up at me, baring her teeth in order to score back some of her pride. "You're terrified of her."

Frothy Poppy?

With her indignation and brattiness and her heart so big it swallowed me whole?

Yeah. I was fucking terrified.

Terrified that she was telling herself some fairy tale about who I was and what we could be. Terrified that she was pregnant.

I ignored Eden and made a promise to myself. To Poppy. I would get her out of this. Out of this marriage. This fucking city, if that's what it took. I would get her far, far away from me.

"You want me to take them a message?" Eden said, looking to be useful until the very end in the hopes it would keep her alive.

"Tell them I'll come to them. They send one guy to my door and this whole thing goes to shit."

"It doesn't really work that way with the Morellis," she said with a wince.

"It does with me. They want the missing Morelli, they get him on my terms."

I set down my glass and walked over to her, close enough that she leaned back in her seat, and I put my arm on the back of the banquette like I had less than an hour ago when I was fucking Poppy like I might die without her.

"And if any Morelli, including you, comes near Poppy, I'll kill them."

✧   ✧   ✧

Poppy

"POPPY?" RONAN'S VOICE pulled me from sleep and my eyes blinked open. A headache pounded and my mouth was dry and sticky.

For a second, one blissful quiet second, I didn't remember anything. I looked around the dark and quiet cabin and wasn't sure where I was.

"We've landed," Ronan said. He stood in the doorway, the brightly lit main cabin of the jet behind him. Eden was there in her fur and red lipstick, packing up her purse. And it all came back to me. The Morellis and the Constantines. The strange uncertain future.

My husband.

My porn-worthy wedding night.

A blush incinerated my entire body. Whatever courage desperation and booze had given me, it was long gone. And I felt foolish.

45

"Are you all right?" he asked with concern that, a few hours ago, I would have begged to have thrown my way. Right now, slightly hungover and scared, I was over it.

"Fine," I said and stood up. I wore one of his dress shirts with a pair of women's yoga pants I found in a drawer and refused to think about who they belonged to and how they might have arrived in Ronan's jet. I shoved my feet into the boots I'd been wearing and pushed my hair, snarled from sleeping on it wet, out of my eyes.

"Let's do this," I said. I followed Ronan out into the early dawn of NYC. The city behind us was just waking up, pink-cheeked and fresh. There were two black town cars waiting on the tarmac, back doors open. The air was cool and I shivered in my husband's dress shirt. He slipped his jacket over my shoulders and I wanted to reject the gesture and the comfort but it was warm and smelled like him. I pulled it over my chest. A cocoon of Ronan.

"Well," Eden said to Ronan. "Don't take this the wrong way, but I hope I never see you again."

"The feeling is mutual," he said, stone cold.

"You, however…" Eden hugged me. "You get tired of this man pretending he's not crazy about you and I will be back in an instant."

"Where are you going?" I asked into her hair, awash with surprising affection for this woman who literally blew up my life.

"One quick reckoning for my sins with Bryant and then…" She tilted her head. "I don't know. Eastern Europe? Maybe I can find an old count with a castle somewhere who needs a wife to blow his mind and spend his money."

"If anyone can find him, it's you," I said and then squeezed her one more time. She was born in the wrong time. I could easily imagine her in some medieval royal court, keeping secrets and dispensing poison. "Stay safe."

"You too," she said, and with a wave of her fingers she climbed in the back of one of the town cars and it drove away.

"Are they going to kill her?" I asked Ronan without looking at him.

"I hope not."

Slightly stunned by what passed as an emotional outburst from the man, I turned to stare at his profile. His cold beauty was familiar, it held no new torture for me. But there was something else in his eyes and the corners of his mouth. Something softer. Contemplative.

That would be the end of me. I would see what I wanted—affection and concern when it was just exhaustion. Or gas. I had to remember that, to not go falling in love with what I wanted to be true.

Ronan's hand touched my back and he gestured to the open door of the other town car. Doors again.

I wondered bleakly where this door would take me. What bitter world it opened up. I climbed in, surprised to see another person in the back seat. A young man with light brown skin and deep black hair. "Ma'am," he said with a thick Irish accent.

Ronan swept in behind me. "Raj," he said to the boy and held out his hand.

"I got ya the phones." Raj put two new iPhone boxes in that hand. Ronan handed one to me. "Set them up, programmed a few numbers into them. You can call each other. Me." Raj smiled at me. "You can call your sister."

I clutched the phone to my chest like a lifeline. Ronan had given him those instructions. To put Zilla's number in the phone. *Stop it, Poppy. Stop seeing care where there's only expedience.*

"Thank you," Ronan said, his voice different as he talked to Raj. Brusque and commanding. "The other instructions?"

Raj's eyes drifted from me, back to Ronan,

back to me. "It's fine," Ronan said. "Poppy knows what we're walking into."

"I brought on the lads you asked for," Raj said. "Twenty new soldiers. All of them clean. Niamh gave me their names."

"That's good."

"The house has been silent. Though Caroline Constantine's new killer drives by once a day, real slow, window rolled down. Swear the fucker is just looking for a bullet between the eyes."

"Don't be provoked," Ronan said.

"She's put a bounty on your head," Raj said.

"What? Why?" I cried. We'd known while in Ireland she was looking for him. But a bounty?

"She's just yanking on my leash," he said. "Reminding me who owns me."

"Just so I'm clear," I said. "I'm wanted by the Morellis dead or alive and now Caroline wants *you* dead or alive?"

"Oh no," Raj jumped in to clarify. "She wants him alive."

"What a relief," I said sarcastically.

"We're safe," Ronan said to me without any comfort. "The marriage made us safe."

Raj's eyes went wide. "You're married?" he asked with a smile and Ronan nodded. The ring on my finger felt like a chain. "*Maireann croí*

49

éadrom i bhfad," Raj said, and Ronan's lip twisted in what could not be mistaken for a smile.

"What does that mean?" I whispered.

"A light heart lives long," he said, and I couldn't help it. Wild laughter burst out of me. Raj's smile faded and Ronan turned to look at me with his cold face.

"Come on," I said, punch-drunk from exhaustion and stress and…everything. "You gotta admit that's funny."

His face told me he didn't need to admit anything. "Any other updates?" Ronan asked Raj.

"That lawyer you wanted us to keep tabs on?" Raj said.

"From Bishop's Landing?" Ronan asked.

Raj nodded.

"Wait, you're keeping tabs on Leonard Bennington?" I asked. It seemed like a million years ago that I went with my sister to Bennington's office after the senator died. He'd been such a quiet little man, his glasses slipping down his nose. I'd been surprised that the senator used a rather unimpressive lawyer from Bishop's Landing rather than a big firm out of the city to handle his foundation's paperwork. But the senator was only predictable in his cruelty.

"I am," Ronan said.

"You were. He's gone," Raj said.

"Gone?" Ronan asked, and the cool mask he usually wore was lifted and he showed real surprise.

"Car in the driveway, keys in the house. Wife and kids have no idea what happened to him."

Ronan sat back, blinking.

"You think he's dead?" Raj asked.

"Maybe," Ronan said. "But who killed him?"

There were only two answers. And they were the same people who were after us. I pulled Ronan's coat tighter around my shoulders.

CHAPTER FIVE

Poppy

I SUPPOSE I should have been used to it by now, how at nearly every turn I was incredibly wrong about Ronan Byrne. But Ronan's "apartment" was the top floor of a four-story brick walk-up in Brooklyn Heights.

Right along the river with views of the city out the floor-to-ceiling windows at the back of the house.

It wasn't a shitty hole-in-the-wall or a sleek sky-rise penthouse apartment. No. It was a goddamn home. With rugs and lamps and art on the wall. He shut the door behind me, locking a complicated series of deadbolts. There was a kitchen to my left, a small galley that was impossibly clean. A pegboard wall with cooking utensils and fancy copper-bottomed pans. In front of me were the windows and the lights of Manhattan, surrounded by the dark moat of the Hudson River. A low sofa with blankets folded on the edge sat in front of a fireplace and book-shelves.

Fucking bookshelves full of books. And I wanted to be mad, because I wanted to be mad about everything. Being mad felt like it might keep me safe. But Ronan hadn't lied to me or misled me. He just never told me anything.

Married to an Absolute Stranger: The Poppy Story.

"It's nice," I said, appreciating the warm paint colors that made it seem cozy at night but during the day with all the sunlight that came in through the windows probably looked sophisticated. He didn't say anything. Just walked through the apartment, opening doors and turning on lights.

"Do you think someone is here?" I asked. More silence.

"Ronan!" I snapped as he came back into the living room.

"Yeah?" He looked at me, his dark hair falling over his eyes. He swept it back with one hand and watched me. "You hungry?"

I was exhausted. Scared. Sore. I wanted to fuck him and kiss him and smack him.

"No," I said. He ducked back into the kitchen and opened the fridge. A smile ghosted over his face. I'd fucked him and he didn't smile at me like whatever was in that fridge.

"Niamh set us up," he said. "I can make you an omelet."

"You can?"

"The monster can cook."

"I never called you a monster." Did I? Maybe I did. I was suddenly surrounded by monsters. They seemed to look a lot like humans. And fuck me like their life depended on it. I really had to stop thinking like that. What happened on the plane obviously would not happen again. Not ever.

"Sit down on the couch," he said. "I'll bring you some food."

"I don't want food." I was being childish, exerting control where I could.

"Okay."

"I'd like to order some clothes," I said. "But I don't have any money—"

He pulled his wallet from his back pocket and handed it to me. "Use the black card."

An American Express Black card. He found a piece of paper and a pencil and wrote down his address. "Get what you need."

I took it all and stood there, awash with uncomfortable gratitude and prickly resentment. "Thank you."

"It's just clothes, Poppy," he snapped, clearly more comfortable with my surliness than my gratitude. God, we were such a mess.

"I'm sorry, but you don't have to do it."

"Stop apologizing all the fucking time."

"Stop yelling at me," I yelled back at him, the words ringing through the apartment. I held up the card. "For that I'm going all in at Armani."

I whirled like I was wearing one of Eden's fur coats and sat down on his leather couch. There was a lamp beside me and I flicked it on. The floors were dark wood with a bright red and green and beige rug thrown over it. Everything in the house looked expensive but also like someone had picked it out by hand. Ronan in this house was dangerous. To me. To my heart. Because I wanted the version of him that lived here, that walked these rugs and picked out these photographs to be real.

To be mine.

I had to remind myself that the version of Ronan when we pulled up to this brownstone, we all came in together—that was the real Ronan. Walking past men dressed in black carrying guns. They looked like soldiers and they treated Ronan like he was their king.

"Quiet?" he'd asked one man as we walked by.

"Yes, sir." That was the Ronan I understood. But now I was buying clothes on his Black card and there were photographs on the wall.

How did I make sense of all these versions of him?

How did I keep my heart from leaping into the arms of a man who fucked me like he needed me to live and now was making me an omelet?

I wasn't strong enough to resist this Ronan. I'd be in love by morning if I wasn't careful.

On my phone, I scrolled through the internet and ordered pants, shirts, shoes, dresses, underwear (thank goodness) and toiletries to be delivered tomorrow. Here. My new home. Our home.

Ronan sat down next to me with two plates of food. Big yellow fluffy omelets with cheese oozing out the middle.

My plate had sliced-up apples on it. I was for a second taken back to the cottage and the farl. One sweet. One savory.

"We should have stayed in Ireland," I said, staring at the food.

He looked up at me, his eyes sharp. "You can't be serious."

"Why?"

"Because there was nothing there."

"Rascal was. The cottage was. You were." The words came out unprovoked and I looked out the window instead of at him. Stupid fucking Poppy. Stupid fucking heart. I had to stop giving myself away like that.

"That's enough life for you?" he asked quietly. Like it mattered. Like my answer had the power to change things. I gave myself points for not looking at him. For not throwing myself in his arms.

"Poppy? That's enough for you?"

I nodded into the silence. Reckless and dumb to the very end.

His laughter made me flinch.

And then despite all my efforts, my eyes were hot with tears. Every tear I'd held back for years. Every time the senator hurt me and I didn't give him the satisfaction of crying. With my shoulder I wiped away a tear that slid down my cheek so he wouldn't see it.

There. That's how he feels. Your longings are laughable. Remember this, Poppy. Remember, or every pain you feel after this is your own damn fault.

"You're only saying that because you're scared." He attacked his omelet with the side of his fork. I wiped my face, brushing away all the tears until they stopped.

My stomach suddenly grumbled and I took a slice of apple.

"I don't think I am, actually."

"You're not scared."

"I don't know, Ronan." When I looked at him, all I saw was how handsome he was. And how tired. Which I refused to feel anything about. "We're on the top floor of a four-floor fortress with dozens of armed guards beneath us. I feel pretty safe."

"You shouldn't," he said. His eyes raked me for a moment, reminding me of the plane. Of his touch. His hunger. But then he blinked and it was over and I could tell myself it was a trick of my heart seeing what it wanted.

Ronan demolished his eggs and I bit an apple in half.

"What are the pictures of?" I asked, gesturing at the framed black-and-white pictures on the wall behind his shoulder. There was a wind-swept dune. A sunrise over a snow-covered mountain. A woman smiling over her shoulder in the jungle. She was beautiful and I hated her.

He looked at them like it was the first time and then shrugged. "Dunno."

"Aren't they yours?"

"No. The apartment came furnished."

"You have someone else's photos on your wall?"

"All of this stuff is someone else's."

There's the stone-cold killer I know. Everything fell back into place, these versions of him. I sighed, selfishly comforted and a little sad all at once. I wondered if he didn't care about his home or didn't notice. And then I wondered which was worse.

"What happens tomorrow?" I asked and then pointed my apple at the window and the day outside. "Or today. Or...next. What happens next?"

"You're going to bed."

"You're not?"

"I will," he said, but I knew he was lying. "We need to figure out what the senator had on both families. How he was working with them."

"Blackmail?" I asked. The idea had been spinning in my mind for a while. In his position he'd have a lot of information. The kind that could be weaponized. The apples had unlocked my hunger and I cut the omelet with the side of my fork and put a piece in my mouth. It was more butter and salt than egg and I approved of that ratio.

"That makes sense for Caroline. She works very hard to control her image."

"What do the Morelli's care about?" I asked. The omelet was too rich and I set down my fork and picked up another apple.

"Power. Control. Money." Ronan shrugged. "Hating the Constantines. They care a lot about that."

"Then the senator had information that would have taken that away?"

"Jeopardized it." He sat back, his plate empty. I saw his eyes glance over at mine and I pushed my half an omelet towards him.

"You're not going to eat it?"

I shook my head. "Niamh has the box from Bennington. I'll go get it," he said.

"He's really dead? Bennington?"

"I don't know. I'll have Raj dig around a little more," Ronan said, methodically making his way through what was left of my omelet. He ate like he was stoking a fire, without enjoyment. Pure expedience.

"He was such a no one. Completely innocuous. I can't believe he was a danger to anyone."

Ronan stood up, the plates in his hand. "We can worry about it tomorrow. You should get some sleep."

"I need to speak to Caroline," I said. He shook his head and took the plates to the kitchen.

"Am I a prisoner again? Do I need to remind you how that didn't work out for you last time?"

By accident, in the doorway between the kitchen and living room, his eyes met mine and I caught my breath. Everything that happened in that cottage was there between us. The chair and the dark bedroom, the secrets up on the hill in the church. The cats. The bath and the whiskey. Then he blinked and just like that the memories were gone.

"We go to Caroline's together," he said. "You're not to leave here alone."

"Ronan. I won't be a prisoner."

"I'm trying to keep you safe."

"You married me. Remember? We already made this terrible sacrifice. The least we can do is take advantage of the protection it provides us."

"Our marriage isn't going to keep you safe. Don't you get it?" he asked. "Eden was right, we're leaving leverage every place we go. You are now a tool someone can use to get to me. There are people out there who, when finding out I'm married, will delight in the idea that they can *hurt* you so they can hurt me."

I opened my mouth to argue but then closed it again. His words rang of truth. The silence around us breathed and there were a thousand questions I could ask, but there was only one that mattered.

"Would it hurt you if I was hurt?"

"You daft fucking girl, don't you hear what I'm saying?"

"Well, you're yelling, so it—"

"You don't know my life, Poppy. You think you do and that's my fault. I never should have taken you to that cottage. I never should have…" He stopped. The words he didn't say were ringing in the silence.

Touched you.

Kissed you.

Let you close. *Well, you did,* I thought. *And now we're here.* "You're an innocent."

"Not so much anymore."

"Poppy, I'm not joking about this."

"I'm not joking either," I cried. We were both standing, exhaustion and terror making me yell. "It only hurts you, Ronan, if you care about me and you've made it—"

He grabbed me. "If you were hurt, it wouldn't hurt me." He leaned forward, his face in mine like he could say these words right into my mouth if he could. Into my brain. "It would *kill* me."

He dropped my arms and stepped away. As far away as he could get from me until he was standing at the windows, looking at the city. I stood there, reeling.

"Despite what happened on that plane, this marriage is not real. As soon as we're able, you will divorce me and walk away. And you will never look back." He turned to me. "Don't get it turned around in your head; we will end."

The ground beneath my feet was suddenly unsteady and my head began to swim. I was tired and hungover and now suddenly so…sad. And I wanted to argue with him. I wanted to change his mind and reveal his heart. But I wasn't capable of the words.

"Hey," he said with his voice low and quiet, like he hadn't just punched me in the gut. "Why don't you get some sleep?"

I wanted to sink into that brattiness I had with him sometimes. I wanted to tell him to go fuck himself. But I wanted him to wrap me up in his arms more. So, I gave up the fight. I surrendered to the moment and this moment called for sleep. "Where?" I asked.

"I'll show you."

Like a child I followed him out of the living room, down the hallway, through the kitchen to a bedroom off the back. There was a king-size bed with a black comforter and crisp white pillowcases. The sun was rising through the windows of the front room, but it was dark back here, the sound of the city hushed and quiet.

"There's a bathroom through here," he said, opening a door to reveal a white-tiled room. This was clearly his bedroom. There was a dresser with a silver tray on top of it, cluttered with watches and receipts. Money in a gold clip. The room smelled like him.

"This is your room," I said, my skin flushing with the idea of lying down in that big bed of his and him lying down next to me. "There's a guest room off the living room." He answered the question I wasn't brave enough to ask. "I'll stay there."

"You don't have to—"

"I do."

I nodded. He kept putting boundaries up and I was too tired to keep knocking them down. And then he was gone, closing the door and leaving me in the hushed dark of his bedroom.

All by myself.

Ronan

I STOOD OUTSIDE her door. My door. Our door. Whatever. I stood on the other side of the door, my hands braced on the wall, forcing myself not to go back in there. Not to lay her down on that bed and wrap myself around her. Protect her from everything that was going to come her way.

"You fuckin' fool," I breathed, my head bent, my hands in fists. This was something worse than temptation. Something I'd never felt before, this crushing *need* for her. I was married to my addiction and I knew nothing good would come of this but still I wanted her.

I pushed off the wall and walked through my apartment to the guest room off the living room where I had a laptop and a desk, one of those ridiculous bikes everyone loved and a double bed that I kept around for the Irish kids Niamh smuggled out of the UK when they get in too much trouble with the law. Raj used this room for a month a few years ago.

Outside the door to the guest room, I stopped and looked at the pictures Poppy had asked me about. I had noticed them but never cared. What did a bunch of black-and-white pictures of sunrises and sand dunes matter in my life? I had the sense in Poppy's life sunrises and sand dunes would rate pretty high. They would be things she needed to be happy.

I tipped the edge of the sunrise and the mountain, making it straight and then went into my office.

Every floor of the brownstone was filled with my men. Not Caroline's. Not Morellis'. Mine. Men loyal to me and to Niamh. There were enough men with guns between us and the front door to make me feel like we stood a chance if any of the Morellis came calling.

I texted Raj, who was a good lieutenant. Followed orders. Understood the job. *All clear*, he texted back.

I sent a text to Caroline. *I'm back*, I wrote, and even though the number would be private, I had the sense she knew it would be me. *You owe me some answers.*

I lay down on the bed, over the covers, the phone on my chest. I remembered the feel of Poppy against my body. The strength in her arms as she held me as tight as she could. If only, I thought, if only I was that strong. And I waited for day to come.

It wasn't even an hour before the screaming started.

CHAPTER SIX

Poppy

THE GIRL IN the shop was talking to me, telling me where the underwear was, pointing to the far wall. But I couldn't understand her because there was too much blood in her mouth. And part of her head was gone. And her pretty brown hair was matted with gore. "Stop," I told her. "Stop. You need to stop."

"They killed me because of you," she said. "And I don't even know you. What's so special about you that I had to die?"

"Nothing," I said, sobbing. But the girl kept talking and talking and so I had to scream to be heard. Scream until my throat was raw. "Poppy?"

"I'm sorry!" I screamed.

"Poppy. Wake up."

There was a hand on my arm and I bolted upright in the dark room. "Poppy, you're safe." It was Ronan. Ronan's voice. His hands on me in the dark, and I collapsed into his arms, panic and fear and guilt cracking me wide open. "The girl," I cried. "The girl in the shop. They killed her because of me. Because—"

"Shhhh, shhh. She died because of the Morellis," he said, holding me tight against his chest. His body was a fire I could warm myself against. "You are as innocent as she was."

That didn't feel true. At. All. "No one else can die, Ronan. No one else."

"They won't. I promise, *a chuisle*. I promise."

He held me and stroked my back. My shirt was sticking to me and my hair was damp with sweat but still I was cold. The kind of cold that would never get warm. I realized I was clinging to him. My hands in fists in his shirt. My hair stuck to his face. He wanted less of me and I kept giving him more. I let go of his shirt, patted down the wrinkle.

"Are you all right?" he asked.

"It was just a nightmare," I said and tried to smile, but I was going to cry again. And I didn't want him here to see it. "I'm okay."

"Poppy—"

"I'm fine. Honestly. I'm fine." I sounded like a deranged chipmunk. But I needed him to leave so I could cry in peace. "Go back to your room."

He was silent, sitting there. I lay down and

pulled the blankets over my shoulder and still he sat there. "Please, Ronan," I said, my voice breaking all over the place. *Leave so I can have some dignity.* He stood and I bit my lip against a sob, missing him already.

He braced his hands on the bed. "I can't be what you want, Poppy."

"All I want is for you to leave—"

"Stop," he said quietly. "We both know you want…more. You want a regular life with a regular man. And I'm not that man. I can't give that to you."

I didn't want that. I didn't want it at all. I wanted him and I wanted our life, the kind we could make. In my silence he must have found the agreement he wanted, he stood and opened the door, letting in a slice of light.

"Ronan?"

"Yeah?"

"What if I'm pregnant?"

I heard him stop breathing. I could practically hear his heart stop. The nightmare was gone and so was the adrenaline and I was back to being exhausted. His silence stretched and stretched and I knew he didn't have an answer, either.

I told myself to stay awake, but my eyelids were too heavy.

If he answered, I didn't hear it.

✧ ✧ ✧

Ronan

"WHAT'S THE CRAIC, then?" Niamh asked, making us tea in her shabby little kitchen. She had the good shortbread she ordered in special. It was noon and I'd left Poppy sleeping in my bed like it was the dead of night. If I had my way, she'd sleep through every reckoning that was coming our way, but I knew I would not be that lucky. The only thing I could do was act fast. *What if I'm pregnant?*

"Dead on," I said, putting her off, pretending things were fine. "You?"

"Try that garbage with someone else, Ronan. You look shite," Niamh said, putting the teacup on the table in front of me. I added sugar and milk to my tea and grunted in answer. *So much fucking worse than you know, Niamh.* She sat down opposite me at her kitchen table and laughed.

"That bad, like?" Niamh owned the building and lived in the most modest unit on the second floor. Smaller than mine, without the big bedroom and en suite off the back. But neither one of us had changed our apartments since we moved in. It was my good fortune that the man who lived on the top floor had moved in within the last ten years and had excellent taste. The previous resident of Niamh's was in the early '70s and loved the avocado green craze. Fridge. Stove. A microwave the size of a small car. The table was Formica and sticky as fuck from a million pots of spilled tea. A million more bottles of spilled whiskey. Niamh had given me stitches on this table and set a broken finger. She'd taken a bullet out of McGill's ass before he went to jail. I had no idea why she didn't change it and at the same time I was glad she didn't. Some things were unchanging. Resolute. She was whipcord thin and her silver hair was cut short. Not fashionably short. Like she did it herself with some clippers and a broken mirror.

"Why is there a girl in your apartment?"

"Raj has a big mouth." I drank the tea too fast because I needed caffeine and sugar more than I cared about a burnt tongue.

"It's not just Raj. Word is you're married, but there's no way you're that stupid." I sighed. "You're that stupid."

"We didn't have much choice."

Niamh crossed one leg over the other. She wore jeans and a faded yellow shirt, with buttons and a rounded collar that looked too soft on her.

There were thick wool socks on her feet because she caught chilblains in an English prison and her feet bothered her every day of her life. Of all the women in my life, she's the one I understood the best. I understood her restraint and her self-denial. The way she only used what she needed and kept what she needed to the bare minimum. Niamh made sense to me.

Caroline, when she came into my life, was the total opposite. The wealth and the glamour. The cars and suits and women…it had been a feast for a man who'd been starving his whole damn life. I took it as my due, as payment for years of trouble. Clearly, it had made me weak. I should have done it the Niamh way and kept myself sharp.

"You know," Niamh said. Her mug had a chip in it. A mug that would have been tossed and replaced by Caroline. By Poppy. But this woman kept using it, just avoiding the chip so she didn't hurt her lip. Because the only thing that mattered was restraint and common sense. "I've used that excuse once or twice in my life," she said. "It's not an excuse."

She shook her head at me. "They would have killed her," I said.

Niamh pursed her lips. "Probably not," she said. "Word is she's got some kind of information."

"She doesn't."

"I'm not accusing you of anything, boy," she said, leaning forward, skewering me with her gray eyes. "But you keep telling yourself you didn't have a choice and you're lying to yourself. Lying to yourself makes blind spots and blind spots—"

"Will get you killed. Fine. Yes, I choose her. I choose her living rather than her dead. Is that what you wanted to hear?"

"Not really. What are you gonna do now?"

"Go to the Morellis."

She nodded, approving of my plan. Don't wait. Strike first. Keep the enemy off-balance.

"You have the box from Poppy's house?" This bankers box. "I'll take it to her. But I meant…what are you going to do with her?"

"Get her out of this mess and let her go."

Niamh tilted her head. The kitchen clock, again a relic, was loud, the second hand clicking constantly, like another heartbeat in the room. "What if she doesn't want to leave?" Niamh asked. "There's no room in this life for blind spots."

"I know," I said.

"I'm saying you need to make—"

"I know what you're saying."

"Of course." She shrugged, turning her mug in quarter turns. "There's no rule saying you need to stay in this life."

That actually made me laugh. "What else am I good for?"

"You got more money than most. Seems like you could figure it out."

Poppy and the cottage. Rascal the cat. A dream, all of it. "I'm where I need to be." I stood. "Thanks for the tea and for taking that box up to Poppy."

She waved me off and I stepped from the cracked yellow linoleum of the kitchen into the worn hardwood of the living room with its console television and green and yellow floral couches. It smelled like cigarettes and Niamh didn't smoke. "I had a family once," Niamh said, and I stopped. "Pardon?"

"In Belfast. A million years ago. A husband and a wee boy. Mark. He had a speech thing…" She waved her hand close to her mouth. "Delayed or whatever, and my husband took him every Tuesday to this doctor on the high street. I'd watch them go out my kitchen window. Mark had a yellow mac that was too big and so we kept rolling up the sleeves waiting for him to grow into it but…he was just a wee thing."

I was gut-punched watching her not look at me. "The first time the English brought me in for questioning, they had a picture of my husband and son walking to that appointment. Mark in that yellow mac. And I remember that soldier looking at me and saying 'innocent people get hurt all the time.'"

"Niamh," I said. "I had no idea."

"Of course you didn't. I didn't want anyone to know. But they let me out two days later and I went home and I told my husband it was over. He could have the house and Mark and every penny in our accounts."

"He believed you?"

"I made him believe me," Niamh said, finally looking at me, her gray eyes glassy. "That was my job, like. To make him believe me so he and Mark could be safe."

"Or—" I didn't say it. I didn't say she could have picked her family and left the cause behind. "There was no fucking or, Ronan. Not for me. I'd gone too far by then. There was too much blood on my hands."

I thought of Poppy last night, waking up from that nightmare. No more people can die, she'd begged me. Like I wasn't the one guilty of killing more than my share. Like I wasn't the goddamn angel of death around these parts. I didn't want her in this life. Living by these rules. She was young and rich and she'd seen enough darkness.

"You better go," she said. "The Morellis are not people you keep waiting."

CHAPTER SEVEN

Poppy

MY ENGAGEMENT RING from the senator, I'd left sitting in my house, on a small dish I used for rings on the counter of my bathroom sink. It had been a one-carat emerald-cut diamond. Nothing too fancy or big, as if to enforce his image of a dutiful public servant. He told the press that it was an heirloom, but that was a lie.

The wedding band had just been gold.

He'd wanted something with a little more flash, but I'd picked out the wide gold band. Something about the promise embedded in a wedding ring made me want to be serious about it. Austere. Contemplative, if a ring could be contemplative.

This thing, though.

This giant ugly Morelli ring that weighed ten pounds and was a half-size too big so it slid around, the setting on the diamonds cutting the tender skin between my fingers, there was nothing contemplative about this ring. It was a mission statement. Nearly a threat. I could have it sized, get a blood-red manicure and it might actually look good on my hand.

My stomach growled and I had no idea what time it was. The midday sunshine streamed into the living room, falling onto piles of boxes and bags stacked by the couch. The clothes I ordered.

Normally, I did not give a shit about clothes, but having spent three days in flannel and sweatpants that belonged to other people, I was a little giddy at the thought of something pretty to put on my body. "Ronan?"

"Not here," said a voice from the kitchen and I jumped, turning to face a tall woman with short silver hair and gray eyes.

"Do you know where he is?"

"Cleaning up his mess, I reckon." She eyed me like I was a dog who'd tracked in mud. Like I was the mess.

"You must be Niamh?" I said, using the pronunciation Ronan used with the V sound.

Whatever I'd been expecting, some version of Sinead at the cottage? A rumpled grandmother with wild, untamed hair and a soft spot for rascals? That was not the woman standing there.

There was more of an *I'm willing to do hard time if I have to* vibe about her. She had hair so short it was nearly a buzz cut and a scar across her lip. "And you're the guest." She walked into the living room like a general commanding her troops. "We haven't seen one of you here before."

"A guest?" I asked.

"A weakness," she answered. "Ronan's worked hard to not have any of those."

Oh, she did not like me. *Well*, I thought, *get in line.* "Which mess is he cleaning up?"

"He's gone to the Morellis."

Without me? My eyes went wide with outrage. Of course he did that. Of course he went off on his own after demanding I do nothing by myself. Sit around here like some kind of damsel in distress waiting for him to save me. Fuck him.

"I brought you the box." Niamh pointed back out to the stacks of bags. Beyond them, on the coffee table in front of the couch was the bankers box that the lawyer had given me and I'd pushed into the shadows the night Theo tried to kill me and Ronan took me to Ireland. It was damaged by water and the lid was crumpled on one side. There was soot from a fire across one whole side. It was absolutely miraculous it hadn't been destroyed.

"I brought in that other shite, too," she said, talking about all my new things.

Faced with her austerity, being excited about new clothes felt impossibly frivolous. Niamh gave me the sense she'd never be inconvenienced by a lack of underwear. Ronan had said she'd had to leave Ireland or face charges, and I imagined her in the IRA, holding a machine gun in the window of some church, firing at English soldiers. There was badass and then I imagined there was Niamh.

"That box sure doesn't look like much," she said as she kept walking through the apartment like she knew it by heart. Years of familiarity with Ronan and his home and I was the stranger. The odd man out.

"I doubt it will be of much use," Niamh said. "A whole lot of trouble for nothing."

Oh. All right. I see what you're doing. She wasn't talking about the box. She was talking about me. And old me would have let this all go, I would have smiled and played nice and let her feel superior to me. Old me was lost in that store in Carrickfergus.

"If there is something you'd like to say, why don't you say it?" I crossed my arms over my chest. Her eyes flashed with surprise.

"Well, look at you, a backbone and everything."

"Say your piece and go," I told her. "I have messes to clean up, too." She stepped closer to me and I did not step back. I met her eyes and held my ground because I hadn't done anything wrong. She could be mad at me all she liked. It's not like I wanted any of this. Well, except Ronan. I wanted him plenty.

"Manage your business and get the hell out of here," Niamh said, her voice thick.

"We're married, did he tell you that?"

"He did."

"A church and everything."

"His hand was forced," Niamh said. "Not sure why you're proud of it. You'll get that boy killed."

I wanted to argue, but her words had the terrible ring of truth to them. There was a good chance I would get him killed. The bankers box sagged on the coffee table and I wanted to believe all the answers we needed to spring the trap we were caught in would be in there, but nothing had been that easy so far. "Or worse, you'll get yourself killed and he'll blame himself for the rest of his days."

That made me flinch. "Do you care for him, then?" she asked.

"So what if I do?"

"Do you love him? Proper, like?" I was silent. Some small scrap of self-preservation held my tongue. "If you don't, then leave. Right now. Go out the door and don't look back."

"And if I love him?"

"Take him with you."

Mouth gaping, I stared at her, seeing behind the military aspect of her whole vibe, a woman who might, just might, be lonely. Who might have regrets.

"He said you might need this." She put a bottle of pain reliever on the dining room table and was out the door before I could muster a reply. Get Ronan to leave this life…this world? I didn't know what that would look like…or how I could manage. But even as I pushed the thought aside as ridiculous fantasy, I imagined us back in Ireland. Our own garden. Our own cat.

Is that enough life for you?

The question was, was that enough life for him? I remembered the sharp edge of his laughter when I'd answered yes to his question and could only surmise—no.

That wasn't a life he wanted. So, it was back to this life we were in.

I stared at the sun making its way across Bennington's bankers box and considered my options.

Ronan was gone. Off to see the Morellis without me, sure that I would be an obedient wife and stay where he'd told me to stay. Niamh certainly expected me to curl up with that crumpled box that I doubted had anything of use inside of it and wait for Ronan to come home with all our problems solved.

Or I could do what my gut was telling me to do.

Get my own answers.

From Caroline Constantine.

CHAPTER EIGHT

Ronan

BRYANT MORELLI WAS like a million other men I'd met over the years. A bully who'd never been stopped. A soldier who was still standing miles from the battlefield, so he figured he must have won the war. He was pompous. Arrogant. And believed he was untouchable, all of which meant he had holes in his security large enough to drive tanks through.

I parked at the bottom of Bishop's Landing, hiked up the hill, through the woods and strolled into his Bishop's Landing kitchen like it was my own. I avoided a maid and a housekeeper and grabbed a bright red apple from the bowl on the counter. The house was dark and massive. Empty rooms and empty hallways. Rumor was the Morelli children tended to avoid their family home.

This empty house seemed proof of that.

Interesting.

The first floor had a kitchen, a grand dining room where I imagined the Morellis fought their way through the holidays. A living room with big windows and thick leather couches. All of it was dark. Oppressive. Ugly.

Finally, an office. I sat down behind Bryant Morelli's mahogany desk loaded with all his important documents and waited for him. Within ten minutes he came in, dressed in tennis whites and barking into his phone. "Tiernan," he said. "I don't give a shit. Find him. Find the girl. Bring them—"

He turned and caught sight of me, feet up on the desk. My eyes glued to his, I took a large bite of the apple.

"I need to call you later," Bryant said and hung up the phone, throwing it onto the drinks cart along the buffet. I chewed and swallowed and let him look at me for a long time.

All while I got a good look at him.

My uncle.

I never had one of those before.

Bryant was a good-looking man. Deep into his sixties but he looked plenty younger. Fit. Strong. All his hair, black with silver sprinkled through it, still on top of his head. We had the same nose, as much as I didn't want to see it.

Same shape to our eyes.

I looked at him and felt nothing. Absolutely nothing about being a Morelli and sharing a bloodline with this asshole. Less than nothing. My bloodline was already rubbish from my da's side. What was a little Morelli thrown in going to do to me?

What if I'm pregnant?

The thought sent a cold chill all the way through me.

"How did you get in?" Bryant finally asked.

"Through the kitchen."

"Are there dead bodies on my lawn?"

"It's not that kind of visit," I said. "But I didn't see anyone except a maid and a housekeeper."

"I need to have a word with my security detail."

I took another bite of apple.

"Would you like a drink?" he asked, gesturing to the cart. "The return of my long-lost nephew seems like the kind of occasion we should toast to."

"Only if you're a Morelli."

"I hate to break it to you, Ronan, but even if your birth certificate didn't say it, I'd know you were Gwen's son. Truthfully, I can't believe I didn't see it before." He poured two fingers of the good stuff and walked across the room to set it on the desk in front of me. "You look just like her." He poured himself the same and then gestured to his face. "It's your eyes. And the way you look at me like you'd kill me if you had half a chance."

"My mother looked at you like she wanted to kill you?"

"She looked at all of us that way. Regrettably she was born with a conscience that my father could not beat out of her. And he really gave it his all." He shrugged. The implications of his words would not move me. Though it seemed my mother and I had abusive asshole fathers in common, too.

"How much do you know about her?" He sat down across from his desk like the power I'd taken by sneaking in and sitting at his desk didn't matter to him. As a gesture, I quite liked it. I just didn't have time for this bullshit.

"I'm not here to talk about my mother."

"Of course, you are." He smiled at me like he knew me and I took another bite of his apple and stared at him until he blinked. "Humor me," he said, tilting his head.

"She got tired of being a Morelli and left. Met my father in London. Had me. Died."

"Oh, that's only part of the story, I'm afraid. She was tired of us and of being a Morelli her whole life, but she did enjoy being rich. She didn't leave until she fell in love with a boy my father did not approve of. Came home from some carnival with a diamond ring and a plan to run away with him. Her mistake was telling my father." He took a sip of his bourbon and sighed. "The boy was killed and Gwen vanished. She wanted to be an artist or some bullshit. Truthfully, I barely paid attention."

I resisted the images that unspooled in my head. The vision of my mother not as a faceless Morelli but a person wounded by them. In love with someone torn away from her.

A woman so conditioned to unhappiness, my father seemed like home.

"Why did you want Poppy dead or alive?" I asked.

"Right to brass tacks, I've heard that about you. You"—he pointed his finger at me over his cocktail—"did not make that easy for me in Ireland. Some of the best-hired guns in the world and you got yourselves out of it. Almost made me proud."

"Why did you want Poppy dead or alive?"

"Who would have guessed Caroline's little pet

would be so elusive? Or, if Eden's wedding pictures are the real deal, she's your pet now. You have to be careful of those Constantine types. They'll smile to your face and stab you in the back, wedding ring or not."

I kept my mouth shut and promised silent bloody revenge while Bryant sipped from his tumbler and then smacked his lips. The asshole thought he was toying with me. I put my apple down in the middle of his desk, the juices dripping all over his important shit.

"You can believe the pictures," I said. "Now answer my question."

"Well, alive would have been ideal. But dead was not an insurmountable obstacle."

I picked up my glass and heaved it across the room. It smashed spectacularly against the wall a few feet from his head. Bryant flinched, wiped bourbon off his cheek. And then smiled at me. Like my violence was further proof we were kin.

"Answer the fecking question."

His eyes widened slightly and he lifted his hand. "I believed she had information regarding the Morelli family and property belonging to the Morelli family that I would like back."

"She doesn't have anything."

"Well, it seems she has you," Bryant said,

smiling at me. "The Bulldog is on the end of someone else's leash. I imagine Caroline is distraught."

I stood and Bryant had the good sense to recoil in his chair.

"The senator was doing some…work for us."

"What kind?"

"The sensitive kind. The expensive kind. But, this is all water under the bridge," Bryant said, crossing his legs, waving his hand like his hunting Poppy down was nothing to be concerned with. "We're family now. Let's consider it a wedding present."

I laughed in my throat. Wedding present? This guy was so full of shit.

"No? You aren't interested in my gifts?" Something in his eyes got dark and hard and this man, I recognized. The evil in him. Rich. Poor. It didn't matter. Men like him were all the same at their core. "Then how about this? Let's call it a retainer."

"For what?"

"For you. For your…services." Bryant smiled in that way of rich men who were used to getting what they wanted.

My skin was suddenly too tight. Perhaps I should have expected this. He wanted violence. I wanted peace. "Why are you the one doing the hiring? Lucian is the CEO of Morelli Holdings."

He scoffs. "On paper, perhaps. The board thinks they can use him. He's a weapon in my arsenal, but I still control the family. And without having to babysit Morelli Holdings, I work on my own businesses on the side." I knew all about Lucian and Leo. It had been a part of my job, knowing as much as I could about the Morellis. The family was fractured. Lucian had taken over the business. Leo had built his own small empire. The father was getting pushed out. "What if I don't want to work for you?"

"Then we might have trouble."

"Trouble is my business, Bryant. I'm not scared of trouble."

"You already sound like a Morelli."

"What about the lawyer? I am guessing you had something to do with his disappearance as well?"

"What lawyer?"

"Don't be stupid, Bryant."

"That Bishop's Landing man?" Bryant shook his head. "He's a minnow, Ronan. I'm after bigger fish. You, namely."

I walked around the desk towards the door, leaving my apple and my uncle where they sat.

"Don't get up," I said. "I'll see myself out."

"Ronan." I heard him get to his feet behind me. Against my better sense I turned. He stood there in ridiculous tennis whites, surrounded by so much wealth and privilege it was like he was on a different planet. "I know you're struggling with it right now. But you are a Morelli, It's in your blood. It's in your temper. The way you fight. The way you survive. You're mine, son. Come, take your rightful place at my side. I can make you a king."

I thought of the way my temper leaped every time Father Patrick called me son. How it grated against my soul. This man, this blood relative, said it and I felt nothing.

I didn't want to be a king. But a man like Bryant would never understand that. He thought he was the envy of all men.

"I am not," I said. "I'm Gwen's son and you fuckers broke her heart and kicked her out." I thought of my da, the kid next door with the skateboard. The priests. Tommy. All of it added up to something small and sad. "I am no one to you."

Bryant's smile vanished and his face was hard and cold. The patriarch of a family that eats its own. "Refuse me, Ronan and I'll be forced to bring Poppy in for a conversation. As the senator's beneficiary I'm going to need what I paid for, or my money back. And…you know how those conversations go, don't you? I think you've been the one asking the questions a time or two."

"Are you that crazy?" I asked. "To be threatening my wife right in front of me? I could kill you right now and the only one who'd hear you scream is the goddamn maid."

He stepped back, his hands up. "I apologize," he said. "If you change your mind about Gwen, I have a box of hers around here somewhere. Art and pictures. Nonsense really, but as her son—"

I slammed the door behind me as I walked away.

CHAPTER NINE

Poppy

"**R**ONAN WILL NOT like this," Raj said for the millionth time. He was with me in the back of the town car as we left the city behind on our way to Bishop's Landing.

"Calm down."

"Easy for you to say," Raj grumbled, looking out the window. "He won't fire you."

"He won't fire you either."

"Because he's going to kill me."

"No one likes a drama queen, Raj."

He laughed and looked at me with wide eyes. "You really seem different today."

"The power of sleep," I said. But it was more than that. I'd showered and shaved my legs and used new lotion and makeup. My hideous hair was still hideous. But a little product made it look slightly better. Like I'd made an edgy choice I couldn't quite pull off rather than having been attacked by a raccoon in my sleep.

I relished my new underwear, sexy and lacy and far more fancy than I usually wore but I was going to enjoy a lingerie renaissance. Not only because it made me feel good but I liked thinking about Ronan seeing me in this underwear.

I liked imagining the clench of his fists as he tried to resist me. And then the way he'd tear it off me when all his efforts at resistance failed.

This won't happen again. Yeah, I'd like to see Ronan try to say that once he's seen the strategically placed pink bow on my knickers. Over the black lace and silk, I dressed in black linen palazzo pants and a bright red silk tank top.

The scar on my shoulder, healing nicely, was on full display. It looked badass, I thought. Caroline would find it horrific and that was part of my plan. Look at me, I was saying. Look at everything that's happened and I'm still standing.

I'd slipped my feet into wedges that gave me a few inches. And the person I looked at in the mirror was put together and confident. And, a little bit, a stranger. I liked her.

When we rolled up to the gates of the Constantine compound, I unrolled my window and leaned out to talk to the armed guard.

"Tell Caroline that Poppy is here to see her. Poppy Byrne."

"Do you have an appointment?"

"I don't need one." I rolled the window back up and within seconds the gate was sliding open and the town car eased its way through the old-growth oak trees that lined the drive. Despite not wanting to, I remembered climbing those trees with my sister and Winston Constantine before he was too old to play with us.

My hands in my lap shook with sudden nerves and deep rage. Past the last tree, the front of the house appeared with its marble steps and Corinthian pillars. And there like a Greek goddess secure in her kingdom was Caroline. Blonde and beautiful as ever, her face making the appropriate expression of worry and relief.

Caroline was wearing her signature cream, a pair of pants and sweater. She'd tried so hard to make me over in her own image. Blonde hair, pale dresses. Young and feminine and forgettable. It was all part of Caroline's systematic control of me, couched in care. In love. In favors and generosity.

But always at the root of it—control.

"You can stay in the car," I told Raj when he reached for the door.

"You're joking. Ronan honestly will kill me."

"Ronan's not here." And I needed Caroline to tell me the truth, something she wouldn't do with a stranger in the room. Caroline controlled the narrative and I was done with the story she'd been telling me. The driver opened my door and I stepped out, watching Caroline every minute. I saw for a second that she didn't recognize the person standing in front of her, and when she realized it was me with new hair and new clothes, a badass scar on my shoulder, her eyes went wide. That was real. All real. I knew that because she immediately covered her honest reaction with a trembling hand pressed to her mouth.

"You're alive," she said, tears in her blue eyes, and man, you had to give the woman credit. If I wasn't looking, if my eyes hadn't been opened to her duplicity, I would have sucked down her concern for me like mother's milk.

"I am," I said, coming to a stop on the bottom step. We were nearly eye to eye.

"Where's Ronan?" she asked, glancing over my shoulder. And then at my shoulder.

"Not here." I saw that register. A slight widening of her eyes. The twitch of her lip like a smile before she hid it.

"What happened?" Caroline asked, reaching for my hands, my scar. "When we heard your driver was killed and you were missing, I had no idea—"

"Stop," I said and pushed her hands away. "Just…stop. We're going to talk, but if you keep pretending like you didn't know exactly what was happening, I'm going to leave and go right to the Morellis."

And like a switch was flipped, Caroline stopped. The tears dried up and the tremble in her hand was gone and she looked at me with new eyes. Wary eyes. "Well, well," she said, her voice colder. "I wonder what got into you. My bulldog, perhaps?"

I nearly laughed. "Are you asking me if I had sex with Ronan? Have you not heard the news, Caroline?"

She went excruciatingly still. "I married your bulldog." I held out my ugly unholy ring. She stared at it, speechless. "Invite me in, Caroline. I have some questions I need answered."

Inside, there was a man standing at the door. Thick neck. Hands tucked behind his back. His eyes locked on the middle distance. Ronan's replacement. Did Caroline pick him up off the streets of some city? Feed him and train him to believe she cared about him even a little bit, only to make him a killer? I doubted it. This guy seemed like hired meat. He had none of Ronan's lethal edge. His keen hunger. His beautiful intelligence.

I took the sweeping staircase on the other edge of the foyer to the second floor and then the smaller staircase to the third, where Caroline's windowed aerie of an office looked over the rolling green hills of Bishop's Landing.

I'd been in this office a million times, the last just a few weeks ago, when we talked about the foundation. When she granted me control of it and I felt so proud. So strong. The version of me then couldn't even dream of the version of me I was now. Caroline's assistant Justin jumped to his feet behind his desk, unable to hide his surprise at seeing me. He at least looked happy. "Poppy. You're here."

"I am. We'll need some coffee," I said. Inside the office, Caroline made her way behind the desk and I realized how she was going to try and recalibrate the power dynamic. She was going to take over from behind that desk because that was what she did. She'd control the conversation, feed me lies and gaslight me into believing her. And that no longer worked for me.

"How much did you know?" I asked before she even had a chance to open her mouth.

"About what?" Caroline asked, and I saw right through her wide-eyed innocent act. God, how long I'd been a fool.

"Let's start with Theo the driver."

"Did I know he was a Morelli hitman? No."

"Did you know the senator was working for the Morellis?"

"No. Though at the end I had my suspicions." She tilted her head, her eyes all over my scar. "You were shot?"

"Are you going to pretend to care?"

Caroline had the gall to look hurt. "I know it might not seem like it where you stand, but I always cared."

"That must be why you married me to the senator," I said, like it all made sense. "All your care certainly explains why you sent me back to him. Your care has been so good to me—" I shut my mouth, tilted my face away from Caroline. I just couldn't stand to look at her anymore.

"Are you forgetting about your sister?"

"What about my sister?"

"You couldn't have handled that situation on your own. You needed help. I helped."

"And I repaid you in blood." I nodded my head. "That's your barter and trade system, I just didn't realize it."

"You had a choice."

"Don't—" I gasped. "Don't you fucking comfort yourself with that lie."

Caroline's tongue came out and touched the middle of her upper lip. "Fine. You're right. I needed the senator under the control of the Constantines and not the Morellis. He expressed some interest in you and I saw a way to keep his loyalty."

"Well, that worked out great, didn't it? For all of us."

"I didn't think he would"—Caroline shook her head—"actually hurt you."

"Well, that's a relief." My sarcasm was a goddamn delight.

She blinked at me, stunned, and I smiled at her with all of my teeth. "Why did you have him killed?"

"The senator?" Caroline's eyes went wide and then narrowed. "Is that what Ronan told you? That I gave him the order?"

I tried to remember the conversation. Had he told me? Had I assumed and he let me believe what he wanted? Caroline took my silence as a yes.

"No, honey, Ronan went rogue on that one," she said, settling into that old position of hers. I was the child, she was the adult and the world was far too complicated for me to understand.

Fuck. That.

"You're saying he did it on his own?"

"Apparently your bruises were a step too far for my bulldog."

"Caroline—"

"Yes. Ronan killed him for his own reasons."

"Did you order him to seduce me?"

She shook her head slowly, a smile on her face. She was really enjoying this. "Not even I'm that cruel. I imagine he makes the senator feel like a prince?"

Oh, how wrong she was. How clearly she did not know Ronan. But I wouldn't be the one to inform her. To change her mind. "You wanted me occupied. Distracted." That was what he told me.

Her face folded into lines of pity. "He lied."

"Then why…?" I stopped because I didn't want to hear her speculation. I didn't actually want to hear Ronan's name out of her mouth. But the rug was fully pulled out from under my feet.

"I imagine," she said, "that he took pity on you and your bruises and the way you clung to the corner of every room scared of your own shadow. He always was a sucker for a victim."

I flinched and regretted it immediately. Showing her that much. Giving her any more of myself.

"Is that why you have a bounty on his head?"

"No. I have a bounty on his head to remind him who he works for." Caroline got to her feet and I realized I was standing, too. And so the gloves were off; we were done pretending. I was not a child and she did not save me.

"Call it off," I said.

"Why should I?"

I stepped towards her, not only ready but suddenly longing to do violence to her. To snatch out her hair. To bloody her nose. My muscles clenched with a need for action. For blood. After all she'd done to me, to my family, smashing her face against the desk seemed like the least I could do. She must have seen my bloodlust, barely contained. She stepped back and held up her hand.

"Fine," she said. "I will remove the order. But he owes me answers."

"He doesn't owe you shit, Caroline. You don't seem to understand that. We don't owe you anything."

"That's remarkably ungrateful of you," Caroline said, managing to appear hurt by my attitude. Like she was a mother and I was a surly teenager. I felt my temper fraying and surrounded myself with some of Ronan's icy chill.

"Do you know why the Morellis wanted me dead or alive?" I asked.

"My guess is that it had something to do with the senator and the work he was doing for them?"

"Do you know what kind?"

"The bad kind, Poppy. Oh, they have Morelli Holdings to do legitimate business, but they always have something on the side. Especially Bryant." She looks almost wistful. "He can't help himself. No doubt he'll try to pull Ronan in as well."

I recoiled at the thought. "Ronan won't work for them."

"That you can still be this innocent, Poppy, is proof that I did the right thing trying to protect you."

"Protect me?"

"I know you don't trust me. I understand that, I do. But everyone has a purpose. And you were no exception. But everything is different now. Ronan is a Morelli."

"Ronan won't hurt me," I said, sure of that, at least. He'd killed the senator because he hurt me. He seduced me because he'd been unable to stop himself.

If you were hurt, it would kill me.

I wanted to take these three truths and study

them, roll them in the sunlight and add them up, but now was not the time.

"You," I said with a shrug. "I'm not so sure of."

She grabbed my hands and I was so stunned I let her. "Take everything out of your accounts and leave. For your sake and your sister's. Don't tell anyone where you're going. Especially not Ronan. Just disappear."

Leave Ronan? He was the only one who treated me like I mattered.

He'd killed the senator because he hurt me. Seduced me despite knowing it might cost him everything. Married me to keep me safe. My heart lurched forward, straining at all the leashes and chains I had around it.

"Did you know who Ronan was?" I asked Caroline. "In Ireland? Is that why you brought him here?"

"You mean did I know he was the missing Morelli?" Caroline asked and then nodded. Even suspecting it, I barely managed to swallow my gasp of surprise. Caroline was playing the long con and had been for years. "I had Gwen followed. I would have thought the Morellis would have done the same, but when they disown someone, they mean it."

"Eden Morelli knew," I said.

"She was always the one to watch for in that family. The only one with a modicum of intelligence."

"That's why you brought Ronan here?" I asked.

Something happened on Caroline's face, like the mask she wore, not just of compassion or kindness but of the total sum of her humanity, fell away. "Was I supposed to leave him, Poppy? A Morelli as a petty thief? A part-time hustler? All that brilliance wasted? When I could raise him up as my own? The perfect trump card."

I shook my head, disgusted with her. With every bit of her and all the times in my life I believed her lies.

"Now he's mine. And you won't touch him, Caroline. You don't have any power left over him. Send your meat puppet down there and Ronan will kill him for breakfast. And if he doesn't, I will."

"You're not this person, Poppy," Caroline whispered.

"You don't have the slightest idea who I am."

I left without saying goodbye. Without a single other word. Remarkably, I came in here without a purse. Or a coat. No bag. Just myself.

And I still walked out of there feeling like I'd shed something. Left something behind. Something heavy and cumbersome. Raj was standing by the car looking nervous. "Everything all right?" I asked when I approached.

"Your phone was blowing up," he said as I climbed in the back seat. "It was Ronan. I didn't answer. But then he called me."

"You told him where we are?" He nodded and winced. I grabbed my phone and called Ronan, hoping I could get him in time before he unleashed a war on Caroline Constantine.

"The fuck, Poppy!" Ronan yelled, answering before the phone even rang. "You went to the Constantines alone? Are you all right?"

"Fine. I'm fine. All is…fine."

"I'm coming to Bishop's Landing," he said. "I've got twenty men—"

"Stop. Call off your men." We pulled away from the Constantine compound, leaving it in my rearview mirror. "I'm coming home."

CHAPTER TEN

Ronan

THIS WAS COMPLETELY fucking unacceptable. Completely out of bounds. I paced from the window with its view of the city, past the door and the kitchen, down the hall to my bedroom and back. What was needed here, clearly, was a reestablishment of the fucking rules. I said stay and Poppy stayed. Those were the fucking rules. And now, well, there would be punishment, wouldn't there? On her head. On her fucking head. Going off to the Constantines by herself, like some kind of…what? I didn't even have the words for this shite.

There was a knock on the front door and I wrenched it open, revealing Poppy and right fucked Raj behind her. Words with him later, to be sure.

"I'm probably going to need a key—" Poppy was saying and I grabbed her hand, pulled her inside.

"Ronan—" Raj started, and I pointed my finger at his face.

"Later," I said and slammed the door.

"Ronan." Poppy pulled herself free and took a step back. "I can see you're upset."

"Upset?" I shouted and then wished I didn't. Poppy loved emotion. She thought she was winning when I showed it. And she couldn't think this kind of behavior would be rewarded. I stepped forward and Poppy stepped back. "I'm not upset, Poppy," I said in a calm, silky voice thick with my father's accent when he was deep in a rage. There wasn't much I could do about that.

"You seem upset," she said. Scared but trying to be cute. I was not, absolutely not, going to love that. I was not going to be moved by her quivering lips or that fucking red tank top that clung to her breasts. Was she even wearing a bra? What was she doing walking around like that? She wore dark makeup around her eyes that made her look young and edgy and so different from the scared mouse I met so long ago. I'd left a sleeping girl with nightmares and opened the door to…some new creature.

"What did I say last night?" I asked her, and she stepped back again. I followed. One step at a time until she hit the back of the couch. "Poppy, what did I fucking say?"

"Not to go. Not to go anywhere. But, Ronan, I'm not a child."

"You're acting like one."

"Stop it," she snapped, and braced a hand against my chest. Like she could hold me at bay. I was a million times stronger than her, worlds harder and meaner. "I'm acting like an adult and you don't scare me."

I knew how to scare her. How to destroy those rose-colored glasses she wore when she looked at me.

Pain.

I smacked her hand away and she didn't look so sure of me anymore. But still that chin came up like she was daring me. I stepped back. "Take off your clothes."

"You're joking."

"Do I look like I'm joking? You act like a child, you'll be punished like a fucking child."

"Ronan—"

"Do it. Or I'll do it for you."

She stepped sideways, trying to get out of reach. "You wouldn't—"

I snagged her around the waist. Too much fucking talking. The tank top she wore was silky and hung from her shoulders by tiny little straps that snapped like string in my fists. She gasped and I got so fucking hard. I snapped the other one and she put a hand to her shirt like a damsel defending her modesty. *I'm going to fuck that modesty right out of her. I am going to defile her seven different ways.*

"What…" She licked her lips, her eyes wide. Unsure. Scared. "What do you think you're doing?"

"Teaching you a lesson." I threw her over my shoulder and she shrieked, her hands smacking my back. She wore silly fucking shoes, so I undid them and tossed them to the ground as I walked back to the bedroom where I was going to tie her down until all this shit was done. I tossed her on the bed where she bounced, her shirt torn, her breasts bare.

"Ronan," she said, scrambling backward, and I grabbed her by the ankle, reeling her into me like a fish. Her pants had wide legs and were made out of linen. "You were scared—"

"You should be scared." I grabbed the waist and pulled, the button pinging off. She screamed and my cock jumped. I didn't bother undoing the zipper. I just tore her pants open.

"You were scared. For me."

"Poppy. Swear to God—"

I yanked the pants off her body, revealing black lace underwear. The breath got knocked out of me. I'd never seen her wear anything like this before. Blatantly sexy. Underwear that demanded to be seen. Appreciated. It was lingerie for a lover and she was wearing it. For me. Bought it thinking of me. Put it on this morning thinking of this. This speechless cataract of a moment.

"What the fuck is this?" I growled, tossing her ruined pants on the ground.

I realized my mistake too late. A man dedicated to hurting her wouldn't be distracted by a lass's fucking knickers. The power shifted and the razor's edge of fear I'd been sharpening in her dulled.

"You like it?" she asked and then rolled over onto her stomach. "It has a bow…"

I saw the fecking bow. Right there at the curve of her ass like she was a present for me. It was pink and made out of ribbon. If I pulled that ribbon, she would be revealed to me. It was so pretty it gutted me.

She was looking at me over her shoulder and then had the audacity to wiggle her ass.

I sat on the edge of the bed and hauled her over my legs. Poppy wasn't dumb. It took her a second to realize what I was planning and she tried to buck her way off me. I held her down with one arm across her shoulders. My other hand cupped the full curve of her ass. Palming it, my fingers slipping between her cheeks. I squeezed her flesh until she squeaked.

"You want to spank me, do it because it's fun," she said. "Not because you have some kind of authority over me and my body."

"Who says I don't?"

"Me. And you." Again she looked at me over her shoulder and I wondered how she constantly had this power. How she took what I wanted and gave it back to me with more. How she took my fear and rage and gave me sexy underwear with bows on it. How was I supposed to live like this?

I moved to shift her off me, to stand. To get space and balance. But she parted her legs and my fingers slipped into the heat and wet between her legs. I groaned, closing my eyes in pain. "I think," she breathed, her voice small and young and I didn't know if she was pretending and I didn't fucking care. All of it worked. The quiver of her pussy against my fingers. The wobble of her tits against my leg. The way my blood hammered through my cock. "I think I like it."

"You're a fucking problem, Poppy," I snarled, slipping my fingers over her clit, making her jump.

"I'm sorry. I don't mean to be."

"Yeah, you fucking do. You're stubborn and you're foolish and you think the world can't hurt you and you wear this silly underwear." I pushed her legs out wide over mine, pulling the lace against all her sensitive parts until she gasped. Maybe with pain. Maybe pretending. I didn't know and I was too far gone. I was hurting, it was only fair that she joined me.

"What are you going to do?" she whispered.

"Put you in your place." I brought my hand down against her ass. She jumped and squealed and her flesh rippled. I did it again, losing my grip on control. On everything. Certainly, on her. I slipped my hand between her legs again as if to make sure she was still with me. She was wet down her legs, and as I circled her clit, she sobbed. I yanked the underwear down below her ass, the red print of my hand satisfying to me on some cellular level.

"You like this?" I asked and smacked her ass again. She cried out, arching against my leg, searching for pressure and friction because she was about to come. "No." I held her hips down, shifted my leg out of the way. "You don't fucking get what you want, Poppy. Not until I say."

"What do you want? Ronan?" She looked at me again over her shoulder, flushed and her eyes blissed out. Wild. "You want me to suck your cock? I will. I'll suck it so good—"

"I want you to promise not to go anywhere without me again."

Her eyes narrowed. That little sexy pout of hers vanished. "No."

"No?"

"I won't make that promise."

I smacked her ass again and she stretched out her arms as if trying to grab onto something. There was no controlling this woman. "What the fuck am I supposed to do with you?"

"You could try trusting me," she said. "Trust me the way I trust you."

I rolled her off my legs, her knees hitting the floor maybe too hard, and I worried I'd hurt her. But she stretched the top of her body against the bed, her knees still on the floor, her ass and the bow arched towards me. I pulled off my belt, the leather making a threatening sound that pulled her eyes to me, wide and suddenly unsure. So my brave girl had a limit. Good to know. I toed off my shoes, pulled off my pants; her eyes wide at the sight of my cock. I stroked it, feeling the orgasm barreling towards me, out of control and unstoppable. "Spread your legs," I told her, and she did, still watching me.

"Ronan?" Oh, the thread of fear in her voice, it made me crazed. "What are you going to do?"

"You said you trusted me." I was mean and I was pushed out of my head by her. She looked at me a long time as I stroked my cock, come seeping out the tip. I wiped it up with my fingers and smeared it on her ass. I did it again and smeared it against her asshole. Her eyes went wide and her breath caught and I saw her wrestle with fear and trust. And just when I thought she was going to say no. Just when I thought she'd remember I wasn't the man she wanted me to be, she smiled at me and then turned away, resting her forehead against her hands. She arched her ass and spread her legs. Complete surrender.

Absolute trust. "Just…be gentle," she whispered.

I fell to my knees behind her. I was too far gone for gentle. For patience. I was the animal she made me. I ripped the underwear off and covered her body with mine. I positioned my cock at the entrance of her pussy and pushed my way inside. My way home. She was swollen and hot and still so tight. She pushed forward, away, and I followed, not giving her the chance to escape. To breathe. She was already coming. I could feel it in her pussy clamping down on me.

Poppy was sobbing nonsense. "Please" and "fuck" and "more." I braced myself tight against her, riding out her orgasm with her until it faded into twitches and aftershocks and she was limp and slick between my body and the bed. "Again," I told her.

"Ronan." Her voice had protest inside of it.

"Until I say enough."

She shook her head and I slipped my finger between her legs, pressing my fingers against her clit the way she liked. Soft and then harder. And then harder still. She bucked against me. I fucked her through three orgasms, the third I had my thumb in her asshole and she was begging me to stop and to keep going at the same time.

"Ronan," she sobbed. The muscles of her back were twitching under her skin as I ran my hands down her spine. "Please. Please come."

This surrender was so delicious, more so because it was the only surrender I would get from her. And…perhaps the only surrender I actually wanted. "I love the way you beg me to come inside of you," I told her.

"Yes," she moaned. "Fill me up."

I was already stroking myself through the

slippery mess we'd made between her legs. Hard thrusts that shoved her body against the bed. I liked that too. She'd been used and satisfied. She was mine to use and satisfy.

Surrender and trust.

The orgasm I'd been fighting off was undeniable now and whatever I wanted...whatever the animal in me craved, my years of restraint were too ingrained. I couldn't make the mistake of what happened on the plane again. Surrender and trust were not mine for the giving. I pulled out of her body, stroking myself until I came in creamy white jets all over that bow.

CHAPTER ELEVEN

Ronan

M Y APARTMENT, LIKE most of the old buildings in Brooklyn, had roof access. When I was young, fresh from Northern Ireland and missing what was familiar, I used to come up here to smoke and look at the stars.

Only there weren't stars in New York City. Too many lights, too much smog. So all I had was smoking.

I miss smoking.

I needed something to do with my hands that wasn't touching Poppy. Perhaps now was a good time to teach Raj a lesson about taking Poppy places she had no business going. But, my heart wasn't in it. I knew how persuasive Poppy could be, the way she blinked those big eyes and stuck out her chin and made stone-cold killers into lap dogs.

Fuck. I couldn't say no to her, how could I expect Raj to?

Niamh tried to make this roof something grand. There were chairs and a table. Plants. A lot of fucking plants. She said, every once in a while, after a little too much whiskey that she missed the green of home. That no park no matter how big in the middle of a city could replace the verdant lushness of Ireland.

It was rich coming from her, who'd preached about the dangers of missing anything. Of nostalgia and attachment.

But I'd taken those words on my tongue like communion. And I'd done it, hadn't I? For years. I didn't miss Ireland. I didn't miss my conscience. My soul. I didn't miss kindness. Or decency.

But now, ten minutes after touching her, I missed Poppy.

Missed her.

I missed the give of her flesh under my body. The softness of her skin. I missed her voice.

She was a flight of stairs beneath me, naked in a bed I'd left her in and I missed her like she was miles away. Missed her like I hadn't seen her in years.

I braced my hands against the waist-high wall between me and a four-hundred-foot drop to the ground.

"Fuck!" I said and then I shouted it.

Clearly, fucking her had been a mistake. And I could pat myself on the back all I liked because I managed not to come inside of her like some randy git, but fucking Poppy would always be a mistake. But right now, night settling over the city, I didn't know if I could stop.

There was the clank of the door opening and I pulled myself together. There was so much to do, so much to untangle to get Poppy out of this web. Work would straighten me out, like.

It always did.

"Raj," I said. "We need—"

I turned to find Poppy coming out the door onto the roof. At the look on my face she paused for a second in the doorway. Uncertain. I'd spanked her, fucked her until she wept, and *now* she was unsure.

"Raj told me where you were."

The moon was out behind her. Brilliant and yellow from the smog of the city. Suddenly and without warning I ached to have her anywhere but here. This dirty violent city that didn't care for how soft she was.

How sweet.

"Do you want me to leave?"

No. God no. Please don't leave.

"Do what you like."

She stepped onto the roof, the door clanged shut behind her.

"It's nice up here," she said. "Did you do this?"

"What do you think?" I asked.

"Who did?"

"Niamh."

She was wearing a pair of jeans and a purple shirt. She looked lovely. Young and innocent and lovely. I turned away, my hands in fists, trying to get a grip on all things I'd let go of since meeting her.

"I didn't think she was the gardening type," she said.

"Niamh is full of surprises," I said. The city was buzzing beneath us. A thousand lives going on as they should. The mundane and the ordinary.

"So are you," she said quietly, coming to stand next to me. I shifted away. Childish but I was clinging to control. I'd been missing her and here she was, darling and fucking stubborn.

"Caroline told me you killed the senator."

Fuck. This reckoning. I knew what she would do, how she'd turn me killing a man who hurt her into a love song.

"So?"

"It wasn't her order. You did it on your own."

I'd known this was coming, from the second I'd told the lie, I'd known she'd find out somehow. And I'd written a script in my head.

"Why did you do it?"

A dog barked. A car door slammed. I thought of the first man I'd killed, the taste of good whiskey over bad vomit. All the ugly shit I'd done.

"Ronan?"

The script was simple. Deny it. If she pressed, lie and tell her I didn't give a shit about what the senator did to her. Hurt her until she backed away. It wasn't a sophisticated script but it was all I fucking had.

Her hand touched mine, small and cold and I couldn't hold on to the ugly shit or the script I'd written. She brushed it all aside with those chilly fingers. And I'd be damned for this in ways I couldn't even see yet, but I couldn't lie to her. Not to brave Poppy.

"Because he hurt you. Because he would keep hurting you. Because you deserved better."

If she would have smiled, I could have walked away. If she'd looked at me like a girl with foolish love in her eyes, I could have found it in me to snarl and destroy her.

But she looked at me with calm and steady eyes. Eyes that had seen some ugly shit. And wasn't scared of it. Didn't judge it.

"She also said she didn't order you to seduce me. You did that on your own, too."

"Aye." I didn't know where all this truth was coming from. It would only cause problems.

"Why?"

"Because you so clearly needed to be seduced."

"Why did you lie about it?"

"So you wouldn't go reading into it, lass. Like you're doing. I'm a killer and the senator was a man who needed killing. That's all."

Now, she smiled at me. "And you touched me, because I needed it. You broke all your rules just because I needed to learn how to be fucked. How to come. How to suck cock and—"

I grabbed her by the shoulders because it wasn't like that. "I touched you because I couldn't help myself."

She nodded, the smile gone. "I feel the same way, Ronan."

"It doesn't change anything. I can't be what you want."

"I don't know, you did all right a little bit ago."

Now it was me smiling, like some lovesick fool. She sighed, like she was just so happy to see me smiling and I wiped the expression from my face. I stepped back. And then again.

"Come on, lass," I said, walking for the door. "We have some work to do."

Poppy

THE BOY FROM the college library, the one I'd fooled around with but never went all the way with, knew all these German words. His grandfather had been German or something. Anyway, the Germans have the perfect word for so many complicated, mixed emotions. Like *weltschmerz*—which means the pain we feel when the world doesn't live up to our expectations.

I understood that particular feeling down to my bones years and years before I was introduced to the word. I thought, maybe, Ronan just didn't know the word for what he was feeling. And I wasn't saying it was love, what he was feeling. No. But it was *something*. And maybe if he just knew the word, it wouldn't be so terrifying. Affection. Care. Lust. All those words I would take. I would take and water and grow and have faith that at some point they'd be love. How could they not?

He killed the senator for me.

I followed him down from that surprising rooftop garden, back to our apartment.

It was midnight or after and the first thing Ronan did was make coffee.

"You should get some sleep," he said. "You must be tired."

"No," I lied. "You're right, we have work to do. What happened with Bryant Morelli?" "Who told you I went to the Morellis?"

"Niamh."

"That's why you went to Caroline?"

"Divide and conquer."

"You're not to do that again, Poppy."

My ass was still sore and probably would be for days. "Lesson learned, Ronan. So? What happened?"

He rubbed his hand over his face and I knew, looking at him, what some of the conversation must have been.

You're not like him, I wanted to tell him.

Just because you have the same last name doesn't make you one of them.

"What did he say about your mother?"

"She was an artist."

"Really?"

"And her father beat her. She fell in love with

some kid her father didn't approve of and he had the kid killed."

"I'm so sorry."

"What are you apologizing for?" he said, pushing away my sympathy.

"Because it's hard to hear that your mother was hurt. Even if you didn't know her."

He set a cup of coffee in front of me and I grabbed his hand. I could feel the tension in his arm, the will to pull away, but he stood there. Letting me hold him in this way.

"He said she was born with a conscience. That she didn't like being a Morelli." He licked his lips and in the hush of the apartment I was sure I could hear his heartbeat. "When I was young and the gangs where I lived were taking notice of me because I was quick and strong and I was trying to resist them, I thought…it was stupid, but I thought, if my ma was watching, I'd make her proud. Keep my nose clean. Stay out of trouble, like."

"Ronan," I whispered, knowing where he was going. "You were a kid. All alone."

"And I'm a man now, aren't I? And my ma if she's looking down, she's far from proud, Poppy. She'd be ashamed of me, because I'm just like them."

"You're nothing like them."

He gave me a pitying look and pulled his hand away.

"What happened with Caroline?" he asked. Back to business. "Tell me everything she said."

"She doesn't know what he was doing for the Morellis."

"Bryant said he was doing sensitive work. Expensive."

"What does that mean?"

"Blackmail? Money laundering? Bribing other politicians. Could be anything."

"Okay…so, what do we do?"

He looked at me a long time. Too long.

"What aren't you telling me?" I asked.

"Nothing."

"Why are you lying?" He stepped away and I stood up, following. "Ronan, you're scaring me. And I'm so tired of being scared."

"Bryant said he'd forget the money the Senator owed him, and he'd forget not getting whatever it was his money paid for—"

"If?"

"If I worked for him."

Oh my god, Caroline was right. I gripped his hand like I could keep him through my meager strength.

"How much money?"

"Billions."

I sat back down, reeling. With everything the senator left me, even if I sold all the houses, I couldn't pay that back.

"You can't work for them, Ronan."

"I'm not planning on it."

I took a deep breath and turned to look at that stupid bankers box on the table. There had to be something in that box. Proof? Evidence?

Behind me, I heard the front door open and Ronan was standing there shrugging into a jacket. "What are you doing?" I cried.

"I have to go out."

"Ronan—"

"Trust me, Poppy."

I did not want to. I wanted to scream at him to tell me what he was doing, but I knew that would get me absolutely nowhere.

"Okay," I said.

"I'll be back within the hour."

"Ronan?" He popped his head out from behind the door. "Caroline also said she put the bounty on you to remind you who you belong to."

"Sounds like her."

"I said you belong to me."

✧   ✧   ✧

AFTER RONAN LEFT I sat down on the couch and took the lid off the box and almost immediately fell asleep. Between jet lag, the orgasms, and the emotional overload of the past day, I was useless.

I woke up when there was a noise at the front door.

For a moment I was disoriented. The apartment was dark. Quiet.

Then the noise again.

There were twenty armed guards between me and any Morelli who might want to get in that door—but my heart still skipped a beat. The reality of my life right now was that there might be bad guys on the other side of that door. Or if not on the other side of that door, waiting for me when I walked out of the building. When I went to visit my sister. When I went to buy tampons at the drugstore, coffee on the corner. And I might not ever feel completely safe again.

I hadn't thought of it, having lived my life with fear for a long time. But the fear the senator gave me was different. It was small and hidden. Something I could cover up with smiles and foundation galas. How would I get used to this new fear?

Ronan will show me, I thought, trying to be

comforted by the thought. The lock flipped. Another one.

It had to be Ronan. I knew that in my brain, but it was still such a relief when the door opened and he was revealed in dark dress pants and a white shirt with the sleeves rolled up. His eyes were dark and he looked impossibly tired.

"You all right?" he asked me.

"Fine. You just—"

"Let me in, you fucking asshole." There was a familiar voice behind Ronan and my heart leaped into my throat. I was running towards the door before I was even conscious of it. Zilla shoved past him and we collided into each other's arms.

"Hey," she whispered into my ear and I realized that I was crying. "Hey, oh, Poppy. It's all right. It's okay. Give us some privacy, would you?" Zilla snapped, and because I didn't want to show my fear to Ronan, I didn't lift my head. I only heard him lock the door and walk away into the kitchen. I wiped my eyes, putting on the bravest face I had, but Zilla, as usual, saw right through it.

"Stop," she whispered, sitting me down on the couch. "Don't pretend. You've pretended you're okay enough for two lifetimes. Tell me what's wrong."

And suddenly, it was all pouring out of me. The girl in the shop. Men being killed around me. Being on the run. Being married. So much had happened and I hadn't processed even a second of it. Until now.

Until the comforting familiarity of my sister's arms.

"Is he hurting you?" Zilla asked.

"No. God. No. He's not," I said. I took a deep breath, getting myself under control. "That was just…it's been a fucking week, Zilla. How did you get here?"

"We got back from London like three hours ago and that asshole came knocking on my door." She jerked her thumb back towards the kitchen where Ronan lingered near the doorway, not even pretending he wasn't listening to us.

Ronan went and got her, because he knew I'd be worried. Because he knew I needed her. Something sweet pierced my grief and I took a deep breath.

"Now. Come on. Tell me why you had to get married," Zilla said.

I sensed Ronan and glanced over at the kitchen where he stood in the doorway. Very carefully and very clearly, he shook his head no. *Don't tell her everything.*

I felt another sob rise up in my throat. After getting married, I'd kept part of my life to myself. The worst of what the senator did to me, in fear of Zilla and her vigilante justice and perhaps because I was not brave enough to say out loud the things that happened to me in the dark rooms of my house.

And I appreciated that I needed to keep some of what was happening a secret from Zilla, in an effort to keep her safe. But she was my sister and I was really alone. I told her what I could. Aware every minute of Ronan watching us. Me.

"I never liked Caroline," Zilla said.

"I know. And you were right to not trust her. I'm sorry," I said. "So much pain could have been avoided if I had trusted you and not her."

She pulled me back into her arms. "It's all right," she whispered into my hair.

"I don't know if I would be so forgiving if the roles were reversed."

"You've forgiven me plenty, Pops. We're family. That's what we do."

It felt for a moment, on that couch in Ronan's apartment, like we were young and safe beneath the branches of that willow tree. Safe for the time being. Safe because we were together. But it was as much an illusion now as it had been then.

Maybe more.

Zilla wore a dark skirt that swished around her knees and a pair of black Doc Martins. She didn't have any makeup on and I couldn't help but think she looked so young.

"Hey," she said. "I have something for you. I went by your house before your guard dog over there made me go to England." She cast a narrow-eyed look at Ronan. "I grabbed these." She had a giant purse with her and she pulled out a stack of frames. All my old photos of us as kids that I had on my dressing table. There was one picture of the two of us and Mom, looking glamorous at some Constantine Christmas party.

"Zilla," I whispered. I'd forgotten about the pictures, and now that they were back in my hands, I couldn't believe I would have let these go. The only thing in that house that meant anything to me. "Thank you."

"And this." She grabbed a bulging plastic grocery bag out of her purse and held it out to me.

"What in the world?" Inside the bag there was all my jewelry. The good costume stuff and the very good real stuff. A velvet box in the bottom with the black pearls from Jim's mother. "You grabbed my jewelry?"

"If we were going on the run, I thought we could sell it." Zilla sounded a little sad that we weren't going on the run. I thought of Caroline telling me to leave. To drain my accounts and take Zilla and run. We could have a well-funded escape.

But there was a reason she wanted me to leave. And I wasn't going anywhere until I found it out. I set the jewelry down on the floor with a thunk.

The senator had been fond of giving me jewelry as if it made up for what he did to me. The more of it I wore, the more smug he'd look because it added to the sense that we belonged among the Constantines. Like it was camouflage. He really was such a small man. It was ludicrous that I gave him as much power as I did.

"What did the house look like when you went?" Ronan asked from the doorway to the kitchen. He had his arms braced on the frame, his body tilted towards us.

"Like there'd been a fire, a flood, and a robbery."

"A robbery?"

"Everything has been gone through," Zilla said. "Every drawer, every cupboard. The place is trashed." She looked at me with sympathy, like I cared about those dresses and dishes. The only thing I cared about were the people in this room. And the pictures my sister had brought back to me.

"I'm so glad you're safe," I whispered, grabbing her hand.

"Likewise. That trip to London was no fun. And hey." Zilla turned around on the couch to face Ronan. "What's the deal with the guy following me? Killer accountant? I thought after the senator died he'd vanish."

"What guy?" I asked.

"Eden's man," Ronan said.

"The guy who broke into my room at Belhaven. We talked about it, remember? When I checked myself in."

"That was months ago."

I suddenly remembered Jacob's face in that Red Hook bar when Zilla's name was mentioned. That short, sharp look of worry and recognition. "Eden's been having you followed for a while."

"Well, someone tell him he can stop!"

"I don't mind him keeping you safe," Ronan said.

"I do!" Zilla cried, but her cheeks were all flushed with some emotion that wasn't just anger.

Ronan and I shared a quick glance, and in

that glance we had a whole silent conversation. This was a new trick of ours, born maybe in Ireland, when he'd been unable to keep up his walls. Of course, he'd been reading me like a book all along.

I'm worried.

I know. But I think he can be trusted. And I feel better if someone is watching her. I don't trust the Morellis.

I don't trust Caroline.

Zilla looked at us, her eyes bouncing from Ronan's expressionless face to mine. "What's going on between you two?" she asked.

"Nothing," I said too fast.

"Poppy. You just survived a relationship with a man who would have killed you if he could get away with it—"

"Zilla," I snapped.

"And now you're jumping in with a literal killer."

"I won't hurt her," Ronan said.

"You won't mean to," Zilla said quietly. She turned to face me, and I saw our whole lives in her eyes. The way she seemed to learn so early that the only way to stay safe was to turn inward and I kept reaching for more. More love, more acceptance. More hope.

I went to Caroline time and time again, giving her more chances to hurt me. The same with our mother. It took the senator to cure me of such things. But my sister stood there reminding me that I only thought I was cured. I only thought I was smarter than those old instincts of mine.

That I was, in fact, doing it all again. Giving myself away for scraps. For hope. For fairy tales I wished were true.

"She only loves the things that don't love her back," Zilla whispered. "That's how you'll hurt her."

The problem with having someone in my life who knew me so well was that she knew me so well. I couldn't hide. And she was right. I was very good at loving people who didn't love me back.

But this was different. Ronan was different. I knew it. This wasn't hope. What I felt for him was real.

"Come back with me," Zilla said. "To my apartment. The killer accountant can look after both of us. Or we'll sell that bag of jewelry and buy an RV. Hit the road."

I shook my head. "Maybe when it's over. When we have the answers we need and…" I glanced up at Ronan. "When we're all safe."

My sister looked between us, her knowing

jaded eyes seeing too much. "Fuck, Poppy," she breathed. "You just never learn." There was a sudden buzz from a phone and Ronan pulled his out of his pocket. He listened for a second.

"Does he have any weapons?" Ronan asked, sharpened once again into the killer king I knew. "Take them and let him up." He put his phone in his pocket and pulled—from a drawer in the kitchen—a gun.

"Oh, for fuck's sake," Zilla groaned.

"Go into the back room," he said, walking towards the door just as there was a sudden pounding on it. I grabbed Zilla and we hustled into the back room, watching through a crack in the door as Ronan checked something on his phone. I imagined he was looking at the security feed, and whatever he saw out there did not make him happy.

He glanced back at us and then opened the door, letting in a man whose chest was heaving, the back of his shirt soaked in sweat. He turned as Ronan shifted to shut the door, each of them careful to keep each other in sight. They looked like boxers in a ring.

"Holy shit," Zilla breathed as she saw the man's profile. "It's Jacob."

It took me a second to place him. The man

had the kind of face you never looked twice at, but he was built like Ronan. Lean and wide through the shoulders. Long strong legs. A hard face that was flushed and covered in sweat.

Zilla, before I could stop her, darted into the hallway. "The fuck, man? Are you following me?"

He said nothing, his eyes walking all over Zilla as if he was making sure she wasn't bleeding or hurt. "I followed the car," he said.

"You *ran* after the car?" Zilla asked.

"Only part of the way."

"You want some water or something?" Zilla asked.

"I'm fine."

Zilla stomped off swearing under her breath into Ronan's kitchen a little like she owned the place, which was Zilla's natural state. I heard the water in the sink run and the slamming and opening of cupboards.

"Where's Eden?" Ronan asked.

"Gone."

"She didn't tell you where?" I asked.

"She doesn't owe me that. She paid me. I did a job." Jacob took the water Zilla handed him. He didn't drink it, just took it so she wasn't holding it.

"How long have you been following my sister?" I asked.

"Since your engagement to the senator."

Zilla and I both reeled. "Why?"

"Eden is interested in weak spots. In this case, Ronan's," Jacob said.

"And I'm a weak spot?" Zilla asked, looking slightly…dimmed at the thought.

"You are the weak spot," Jacob pointed at me.

"So why'd you sneak into *my* room at Belhaven?" Zilla asked.

"Because I know what it's like at night in that place," he said, looking Zilla straight in her eyes, almost pinning her in place with his intensity. "And I never saw you as weak. You have more strength than anyone gives you credit for."

Zilla blinked, stunned for the first time in a very long time, into silence. And the killer accountant, who may or may not have run over the Brooklyn Bridge to get to her, blushed. He actually blushed, and this hallway was suddenly too small for the four of us.

"Who do you work for now?" Ronan asked.

"Eden, when she comes back. If she comes back."

"You think she's dead?"

"I think she's scared enough to stay away for good. She'll find another old rich man to marry and move on."

"Will you work for me?" Ronan asked.

A look crossed over his face, something small and painful. "I don't want to kill anyone anymore. I won't do that job."

"What if someone tries to hurt her?" Ronan asked, pointing at Zilla.

"Then they're dead."

"Excellent. You're her bodyguard until all this is over. I was going to have her stay here so I could keep an eye on her, but this is better." Ronan snapped into action, walking back into the living room with all my jewelry in a plastic bag and the bankers box of secrets, and I didn't know how Ronan could just trust this man with my sister, much less everything else.

Ronan didn't trust me.

But he and Jacob were the same, somehow, in some deep, stunted way. Trust was physical, never emotional, because they'd scoured what they could of emotion out of themselves.

Except Jacob ran across the Brooklyn Bridge to get to her. And Ronan…killed the senator.

It really was the sweetest thing anyone had ever done for me.

"Are you sure this is a good idea?" I asked him, following him into the small room where he had a computer and another bed.

"We want him on our side rather than the Morellis'," he said, grabbing what looked like a business card and another phone from the desk. "I called my contact at the FBI and had him checked out. He's Special Forces, black ops. He's been treated for PTSD and depression. Including a stint at Belhaven. He's a killer who doesn't want to kill anymore. And he's in love with your sister."

"How do you know that?"

"The man ran from Manhattan following my limousine."

"And that says love?"

"It says something, doesn't it?" I thought of him and his twenty men coming to Bishop's Landing to save me from a situation I didn't need saving from. I thought of how he married me in that church he hated. How he promised to worship me.

And now he spoke about love? Maybe he did know the word. And just needed practice.

He crossed the room and cupped my head in his hands. "Do you trust me?"

I nodded, the fine hair at the nape of my neck pulled taut by his fingers on my skin. I opened my mouth to say yes, but something else popped out entirely.

"Do you trust me?" I asked, and it was as if I sucked all the air out of the room.

"It's not the same thing," he said. But it was. It was as simple as learning a little German.

"I love you," I said. There. It was out there, where it couldn't be taken back. Where it was real. And had to be dealt with. "I love you so much, Ronan."

In his silence I imagined twenty different outcomes. A dozen things he could say. Some that would break my heart. Most, really, that would break my heart. But a few that would give me hope. That would give us a foundation that we could build on. My heart pounded and tears burned in my eyes and I didn't know how to keep breathing when he was breaking my heart into pieces.

Say something, Ronan. Say anything. But say you love me, too.

Silent, he turned and walked out.

CHAPTER TWELVE

Ronan

I LOVE YOU.

I'd never heard those words. Da certainly wasn't going to say them. The priests were constantly talking about the Lord's love, but those animals had no love in their hearts. There'd been lasses before, but when I got the sense they were thinking those words, I gave them the heave. The closest, I imagined, was Caroline. What I felt for her when she brought me here, had been a profound gratitude. A nearly painful urge to please her. And look where that got me. At best the emotion was useless, at worst it seemed manipulative. A burden.

I love you. I love you so much, Ronan.

I got Jacob and Zilla out of the apartment after a dozen last hugs between Zilla and Poppy.

Poppy's hands were shaking and she looked worn thin. Worn all the way through. Zilla noticed and she gave me a good glaring as she walked out the door.

I locked up the door behind them. I could feel Poppy in the room, over by the windows, trying not to watch me with her heart in her eyes. She teemed with emotion. Vibrated with it. Being in the same room with her was uncomfortable, like one of the priests' little tortures. The smack of rulers across our knuckles.

But I didn't want her to stop. I craved this pain. Hungered for it.

"I'm sorry," she said into our silence. "I shouldn't have just blurted it out like that." *You can't take that back. You said it twice and you can't take it back.* "We can just pretend—"

I turned and she stepped back, away from me. Scared by whatever expression my face was wearing. "Pretend what?"

"That I didn't say it."

I wanted to be savage and clear it all up. Take this unbearable heat between us and make it cold. Make it all familiar, like. Comfortable. But I was tired of watching the light go out of her eyes. I was tired of being the thing that hurt her.

I was tired of the cold.

"Zilla said you only love things that can't love you back," I said, reminding her that she had no business loving me.

"Zilla is wrong."

Her fucking will to believe was painful to witness. And I'd somehow caught it. I was infected with it. With this...hope. And I didn't know what to do with it. Except try to pull it out by the roots, and somehow I couldn't even do that.

"I'm going..." Poppy looked around, down at the box and then the very dark windows. "I'm going to get some sleep."

"Aye," I said, because I didn't know what else to say.

She walked past me to her bedroom and I clenched my hands in fists so I didn't reach for her. I flinched at the snick of the bedroom door shutting.

More coffee, because I was exhausted too, and I sat down at the table with the bankers box. I started pulling out files, organizing them by subject. Houses. The campaign. His will.

In the back of my brain, I must have been ready for it. Her screaming.

At her first shouted, guttural *no*, I was on my way to her.

I found her on the bed caught in another nightmare. Tears on her face.

I touched her shoulders, trying to pull her

from the dream but she fought me.

"Ronan!" she screamed.

"I'm here, lass," I said and pulled her into my arms. She was cold and shivering and fighting me like I was holding her back from what she needed to get to. But the moment she woke from her dream, she quieted. Every muscle still. Tight.

In my gut I knew what she was doing. Bracing herself for pain.

"You were dreaming," I said.

"Yeah, I… I don't remember. It's…gone now."

Were you dreaming of me? I wanted to ask. Was I causing you pain?

She leaned back and I saw the flash of her brave smile in the dark room. "You can go," she said. "I didn't mean to disturb you."

"You're not," I said, settling back against the headboard, my arms still around her. She was stiff, but she didn't move.

"Relax," I said. "It's all right."

Slowly, carefully, she began to melt against me. And the pleasure it gave me was nearly obscene. I'd never been anyone's comfort. I was the bringer of nightmares. Not what kept them away.

"I keep dreaming about the girl in the shop,"

she finally whispered, her hand slowly stretching out to lie flat against my chest. Right over my heart.

"It'll fade," I told her.

"Do you have nightmares?" she asked and it was dark in the bedroom, so I didn't think she could see me when I nodded. But she asked, "What about?"

"I don't remember."

"I can't tell if you're lying."

"I really don't remember. Sometimes I wake up with a taste in my mouth. Whiskey and sick. It's how I know I've had a bad dream."

"Is that why you don't sleep?"

Of course, she'd notice. We'd spent ages together, the two of us. Just the two of us. I was aware of her down to my cells. Of course she'd be paying the same kind of attention.

"Aye."

"You don't have to stay," she said.

"I know."

And I stayed anyway.

"Poppy?"

She didn't say anything, so I was sure she was asleep. It was the only reason I had for saying it.

"No one has ever loved me before."

CHAPTER THIRTEEN

Ronan

S HE'D SLEPT A few hours and woke up just before dawn like a fucking jackrabbit. Ready to go. Full of smiles and optimism.

We'd done an awkward dance this morning around the shower.

"You go."

"No. You go."

And we sat on the couch with damp hair and fresh scrubbed faces and I was tormented by a daydream of fucking her in the shower.

This is what you get spending the night holding her in your arms and listening to her breathe.

And if I'd said, lass, I want to fuck you in the shower, she'd go and turn on the water. And I didn't know which one of us was worse: me for wanting what I had no business wanting.

Or her wanting me.

Either way, I was keeping my distance. I *needed* some distance.

She'd told me she loved me and I'd dried her eyes after a nightmare and I didn't know who I was right now. I was losing my edge and my boundaries and none of it felt good.

Poppy sat on the couch next to the box and radiated hope in my direction. She thought this sad bankers box was going to have some kind of secret in it.

"You already went through it?" she asked, looking at the stacks I'd made last night.

"Hardly."

I had strong suspicions that everything in this box was going to be bullshit. But we had to start somewhere.

She settled down on the couch, a thin wisp of a girl against a dawning day. It occurred to me she hadn't eaten in days. Our clocks were upside down from the travel and she looked like a strong wind could blow her over.

So, I went back into the kitchen and made thick turkey sandwiches with big slices of tomatoes from Niamh's rooftop garden, on good brown bread and brought them in to her. There were more stacks around the box and there was a smear of soot on her chin and across her bright green shirt.

"Find anything?" I asked.

"I glanced through it that night," she said. "When Theo—"

"I remember the night," I said, cold even when I wasn't trying to be.

"I didn't see anything." She grabbed her sandwich with one hand and took a big bite, holding her hand over her mouth as she chewed. She was fucking adorable.

"But I didn't know what I was looking for. I still don't. Bank accounts marked 'dirty laundry'? Maps with a big X on them?" she said, making a joke that I didn't laugh at.

When I sat down on the couch next to her, she shifted so far away there was no way we would even accidentally touch. We were still doing an awkward dance.

I opened one of the dozens of files and found the nonprofit paperwork for the senator's original foundation. And then deeds for homes. Contracts for landscaping companies.

She glanced up. "Thank you for the food—"

"It's just a sandwich, Poppy." Diminishing it despite the fact that seeing her taking such big lusty bites, having her fed by something I made, taking care of her in this small way…felt good. The same way it had felt good in the cottage. The same way it felt good last night, holding her fast against nightmares.

I grabbed another file, but it was just more paperwork for the senator's foundation.

"What happens if we don't find anything?" she asked.

"We go looking for Bennington."

"He's dead, isn't he?"

"Missing isn't dead."

"Caroline said she didn't know anything about what happened to Bennington," Poppy said.

"Bryant said the same."

"One of them is lying?" She looked at me, her mind turning behind her bright eyes.

"Why would Bryant Morelli lie about the lawyer?" I asked.

"I'm not sure he would. Caroline would lie, though, if she had something to do with his death."

"She'd lie," I agreed. "To save face."

"But what if that's a dead end?"

"Poppy–" I reached for her to try and calm her, but she smacked my hands away.

"No. What happens?" she cried. "What happens if we can't get Bryant what he wants."

Bryant only wanted me, but I wasn't going to tell her that. I didn't know how to tell her that.

"I'll handle it."

"By working for Bryant? You'd do that?"

"I don't see a lot of difference between Caroline and Bryant, Poppy," I said. Though that wasn't the truth. But she didn't need to hear any of that. What she needed to hear was that she was safe and that this wasn't her fault.

"There's nothing here, Ronan" Poppy said.

"It's all right."

"Because you say so?"

"Because I'll make it so."

CHAPTER FOURTEEN

Poppy

I WAS SHAKING. A fine tremble that changed the air in the apartment. Ronan was watching me like I was a hand grenade with the pin pulled. Which was only right. It was how I felt.

It was anger in my throat, making me sick to my stomach. But it was something else too. Something I'd never felt before. A need to *do something.*

To hurt something.

I wanted to crush something. I wanted the power to make it all safe for Ronan. The way he would do it for me.

"Poppy," Ronan said, grabbing my wrist. I wanted to snarl and bite him. I wanted to hit him. I wanted to take off his clothes and fuck him until he begged me to stop.

I was rage and violence and…it was scary.

"I'm going to take a shower," I said and pulled my hand free. I practically ran to the bathroom, turning on the shower and grabbing a towel thinking I might scream into it. I wanted…

Ronan was suddenly there. Slamming the door shut behind him. He shoved me against the vanity, his body crowded mine.

Yes, my body screamed. This. Him. Now.

"What are you doing?" I demanded with far more anger than he deserved. But I was full of it and he was here.

"Giving you what you need?"

"What do you think I need?" I scoffed.

"A place to put your rage. Someone to hit. A body to fuck."

I pushed him but he didn't move. Resolute. Rock solid. I shoved him. Nothing. He was strong and big and against my belly he was hard as a fucking rock.

"Do what you like, lass."

I smacked him. Hard as I could across the face. So hard my hand hurt.

His eyes flared, his tongue came out to lick his lips and I was suddenly desperate for his cock. To be filled. Fucked.

I grabbed at his belt, opening it, pulling open his pants. He didn't help, he just widened his stance.

I got my hands around the thick length of

him and we both moaned.

"I won't let the Morellis have you," I said. My fingernails scraped the tender skin of his scrotum and he barely made a face. I could feel the blood pounding in his cock. I could feel how much he liked this.

How much he wanted me.

"You're mine."

He spun me against the vanity, so we were both facing the mirror. God, we were so beautiful. My hair was wild, his eyes burning. I'd never in my life felt so alive. I arched my ass against him and he started to lift the skirt of my dress. *Yes. Now. Like this. Fuck me like this.*

"Brace yourself, lass," he said, his voice a rough growl. His hands over mine on the vanity. And then he was inside me and it was so good. The most right feeling I'd ever had. I screamed with the pleasure of it. With the sweet sting of pain.

His hand came around my throat, lifting my head so I met his eyes again in the mirror. Our bodies shook with each thrust, our hair falling in our faces. I barely recognized myself like this ravaged and ravishing.

"You're a queen, *a chuisle*. A fucking queen."

"Ronan," I gasped, my body alight. And I had

never felt so connected to a person. It wasn't just the sex, it was everything we survived. It was how we were standing here despite the forces that would tear us apart.

Forces that would kill us.

We were alive because of each other and I believed he felt that. Knew it in the marrow of his bones where I knew it.

This is love, I wanted to say. But he was fucking me so hard and so good there was only a high keening sound coming out of my throat. My body shaking, every muscle trembling. I reached under my skirt, my hand brushing the hard length of him as he slid in and out of my body. He hissed and I did it again. I pushed the flat of my hand against him, my heel against my clit and I was lifted up onto my toes.

My orgasm turned the world to glitter, my bones to liquid. My heart more his every time it beat.

"Ronan," I breathed, meeting his eyes in the mirror. "Please," I whispered. I was blissed out and ruined.

I'd removed every barrier I had against him. Every defense. I loved him and he knew it. We were as close as I could imagine two people ever being.

He pulled out of my body, stroking his cock until he came into a towel. His chest heaving.

And I wondered how I could keep him if I never really had him.

CHAPTER FIFTEEN

Poppy

RONAN MADE SOME calls looking for Bennington and I went upstairs for some fresh air on the roof garden. Only to find Niamh in a lawn chair, her face tilted to the sun, wearing a floppy sun hat. At the sound of the roof door opening she looked over with a smile, but frowned when she saw it was me.

Any other day that might make me turn around and leave, embarrassed by her not liking me.

But I had bigger problems and I was climbing the walls in that apartment.

"Expecting someone else?" I asked and let the door slam shut behind me. Something in my tone made her smile.

"Yeah," she said. "But you'll do."

I laughed at the faint praise.

"Where's Ronan?" she asked.

I explained about Bennington and then because she was here and I had no one else to confide in, I told her about the box.

"Nothing?" Niamh said. "Can't say I'm surprised."

"I guess I'm not either. But I was... well, I was hoping."

"Yeah, it's the hope that'll break your heart." She sighed and tilted her face back in the sun.

"Ronan says he'll go work with Bryant Morelli."

Niamh made a sound like "what are you going to do?"

"He says working for Bryant isn't any different than working for Caroline."

"I imagine it might be better. Family, like?"

"Better?"

"What do you want me to tell you, lass? Rich powerful people are the same everywhere." She turned her head to look at me out of one eye squinted against the sun. "What you want is for me to tell you that *he's* different. That Ronan's different."

Yes. My heart leaped in my throat. *Tell me that. Give me that, at least. If he won't love me. Tell me my love has changed him.*

But Niamh was not in the business of comforting me. Breeze ruffled the plants of Niamh's garden. They needed an umbrella up here. One of those tarps that could shield the sun. Give a girl something to hide behind.

"I was a lot like you when I was young," Niamh said and I actually laughed. "No, it's true. I came from a good family. I had a good childhood. My da was involved in the troubles but he kept it quiet. I didn't even know until I was in university. My ma called in the middle of the night, told me that he'd been taken. We didn't hear from him again."

"Niamh, I'm so sorry—"

She held up her hand, not interested in my sympathy. "That's when I started getting involved. Looking for answers. Looking for trouble. Revenge. The whole time I was doing what girls like me are supposed to do. I got married and started a life. I even…" A bird flew overhead and she tracked it with her eyes. "I had a baby."

Knots were forming in my stomach and I wanted to tell her to stop. We were full up with unhappy endings and I was trying to find a happy one.

"But I was slowly turning into a weapon," she said. "A weapon to use against the English. I wasn't born a weapon, I turned into one. I don't need sympathy, Poppy. I made my choices and I live with my regrets."

"Why are you telling me this?"

"Because Ronan was told he was a weapon, from the moment he could be turned into one. He was told his only value was bloodshed. His only worth was mayhem. He didn't make the choice, the choice was made for him when he was too young to have a say."

"And you think if he had a choice, he wouldn't make the same one."

"I've seen the way he talks about you, how he looks at you. He married you for God's sake and he wouldn't take that lightly. I think that boy would kill himself to keep you safe. But it would be nice if people stopped asking him to do that."

✧   ✧   ✧

Ronan

NONE OF MY contacts, legal and otherwise knew anything about Bennington. And I hung up counting it as another dead end. I glanced at my watch and winced. Poppy went up to the roof garden, but this was when Niamh was usually up there. I opened the door to the apartment, to go up and make sure Niamh hadn't made a meal out of Poppy—though, the way that girl was finding her fight, I'd imagine she'd give Niamh a run for her money.

Poppy was coming down the hallway, backlit by sunshine wearing a yellow sundress with ties at the shoulders. Her hair was in clips away from her face. I liked these new clothes of hers. Her new look.

"Any luck?" she asked. I stepped back into my apartment and she came in behind me. She smelled like sunshine and New York and expensive shampoo. Poppy.

"I am waiting for a few people to get back to me," I said.

"So we wait?" I was not comfortable with waiting. Action felt better.

"You want to play cards?" she asked.

"What?"

"A game? Charades?"

"The fuck are you talking about, Poppy."

She smiled at me, a creature of light and dark. Constantly surprising. "Trying to give you some options for killing time while we wait."

"Are you flirting with me?"

"Clearly, I'm not very good at it. We could go get lunch?"

"It's too dangerous," I told her.

"Then whatever will we do?" she asked, batting her eyelashes at me.

"I'll show you," I said and threw her and her pretty yellow sundress over my shoulder.

In the bedroom I kissed her sweetly. Tenderly.

A new kind of kiss. A different taste.

An antidote to the last time. To the violence and the rage.

Our clothes fell off and we collapsed back onto the bed.

"Like this," she whispered, and rolled on top of me. I put my hands on her hips as she fucked me. But it was obvious she hadn't done this before. I imagined the senator hadn't given her any power in the bedroom and at the thought wanted to kill him all over again.

She got the rhythm all wrong and I slipped out and she winced, coming down on me strange.

"I'm sorry," she whispered, embarrassed. She shifted her weight to roll off of me, but I held her hips. Held her there.

"It's all right, Poppy," I said. "Give yourself a second."

"I don't…I haven't done this."

I knew. And I loved it. Her innocence, no matter how fumbling, was delicious to me. As delicious as when she smacked me in the bathroom.

I knew she was not made for war. That what she'd thought yesterday would fade and she'd remember how she didn't want anyone to get hurt. Her heart would return to softness and she'd let go of her dreams of revenge.

I was made for war. Sweet Poppy was not.

I showed her the rhythm she would like, gently. Quietly. It was slow at first, finding the friction and the angle. Shallow and short, not fucking me so much as grinding on me.

I wasn't going to come this way. But she was. And never in my life had that been enough for me.

But Poppy's pleasure was mine for as long as she would share it with me. And it was more than enough.

✧ ✧ ✧

WE LAY IN the dark afterward, exhausted but wired. Every time I fucked her, I felt like I was getting away with something.

She rolled onto her side, our skin sticking together and then pulling apart.

"Watch it, lass," I hissed.

"What did you want to be when you were young?" she asked.

I laughed. "Alive."

"Come on, before St. Brigid's when you were a boy. When you were young enough to have that kind of daydream. What did you want to be?"

"Poppy—"

"It's just a question." She smiled at me. I scowled at her.

"Professional footballer."

"Really?"

"Yeah."

"Were you any good?"

"No. Total shite."

"Are you joking? I can never tell when you're joking."

"A kid I went to school with, his da worked on a ferry between Belfast and Liverpool. I thought… I liked the idea of working on a ferry. Being outside. Coming and going all the time. Being on the water. The birds and shit."

"The birds and shit?"

"You asked, what are you getting cheeky for?"

"I wanted to be a teacher," she said. "I used to line up all my stuffed animals and pretend I was teaching them to read. The penguin was dyslexic. He needed extra help."

Oh my god, she was going to kill me with her sweetness.

"What would you do if you weren't doing…"

she struggled with the words.

"Killing people?" I asked her.

"That's what Bryant will want you to do, isn't it? If you work for him."

I pushed the hair off her face, traced the edge of her ear with my finger. She was so soft. Seriously, the softest thing I'd touched.

"You could do anything," she whispered. "Be anything."

I thought of Jacob in my hallway, saying he didn't want to kill anyone anymore and how, at the moment, I'd thought he was a fool. Believing he could be something else. But I realized now he didn't believe. He was wishing. He was wishing he could be different. And with Eden gone, he saw a way to make the wish real.

I wasn't so lucky.

"I'm a soldier, lass. A killer. War is what I know."

"But it could be different," she whispered and rolled over my body. She was wet and warm between her legs and the weight of her, the *thought* of her made me hard.

She kissed me, sliding down my body to take my cock in her mouth and I tangled my hands in her hair and I let myself wish.

✧　✧　✧

Poppy

"WE CAN ONLY have sex so many times," I said.

"That's not true," Ronan said. He was feeding me again. Pasta with basil and tomatoes and spicy little peppers. A ton of cheese. It was the most delicious thing I'd ever eaten.

"Ronan," I sighed. "Even you need a break."

"Do I though?" He grinned at me. "If it's you crying uncle, lass…"

"I am a little sore," I admitted.

The laughter fell from his face. "I'm sorry, I shouldn't have—"

"Quiet," I said. "I liked all of it."

"So I guess we play cards?"

"I'll warn you, my Go Fish game is legendary."

"Yeah, you're a real card shark. Tom taught me how to play gin rummy. At the church."

"They let you have cards?"

"I figure they thought it was hard to murder someone with paper cuts." He smiled at me, easy and loose in the memory and I hadn't seen him easy and loose in a memory for a long time. "Anyway, gin rummy, that's my game."

"You'll have to teach me," I said. "I don't know it."

A puzzled look crossed his face and he

straightened, looking around. "I don't think I have cards here."

That didn't surprise me. I never saw him watch television. Or pick up a book.

"What do you do for fun?" I asked him.

"Fucking you is fun."

I laughed, the fizzy water I was drinking almost coming out my nose.

"What did you do before I came along." I realized the trap I'd walked into and held up my hand. "I don't mean other women. I don't mean to pry."

"There were no other women, lass. No one who mattered. And no one for a long time."

"So?" I asked, unwilling to let this go. "What did you do for fun?"

"You won't laugh?"

"Oh my god, is it…were you like a mime or something? A clown? Please, please tell me you were a clown."

"Fuck off, Poppy. I'm being serious."

I turned my face to stone. "I won't laugh."

"I used to draw."

Like his mother.

I took tiny sips of air so I wouldn't cry.

"It all stopped at St. Brigid's, but when I was wee, I loved art. I had a teacher who entered a picture I'd drawn in some city contest and it got a red ribbon. I remember even my da was proud of me. Took me to the pub and showed me off."

He twirled his pasta and took a bite. We ate from the pan, sitting at the table. Each of us in our underwear. It was a scene in a rom-com movie and I was giddy with love. It felt like a dream. A bubble I would do anything to keep from popping.

"Your mother would be proud of that," I whispered.

"It was a long time ago," he said. But I saw the wheels turning in his head, the way he might be seeing himself in a different way.

✧　　✧　　✧

Poppy

THERE WAS A pounding on the door that snapped me awake and I registered the warmth of Ronan's body leaving the bed. The hallway light flickered on and Ronan's low voice rumbled. Raj answered. All before I managed to get myself out of the blankets.

Ronan came back into the bedroom, naked and carrying a gun.

"That shouldn't be as hot as it is," I said, watching him put his gun in the bedside table.

"Who was at the door?"

He held a creamy envelope out to me, the kind sealed with real wax. Extremely fancy. Old school.

"What does it say?" I asked, staring at the envelope like it was a snake about to bite.

"I didn't read it."

I took the thick paper and slipped out a note written in a heavy script.

"It's an invitation," I said. "To have drinks with Leo Morelli."

"Me?"

"Both of us."

I wore a red dress with only one shoulder strap. It was tight and sexy and it showed off the scar on my arm in a way that I thought said "I've seen some shit so don't fuck with me."

Ronan was mad at me, but he could not keep his hand off my shoulder, his thumb stroked over the healing edges of the scar sending shivers across my neck.

"You like my dress," I said, curled up against him in the back of the car. Raj was driving. The invitation told us not to come armed and to only come with a driver.

Both of those rules did not make Ronan happy.

"I'd like it better at home."

"You look nice," I said, running my hand down the crisp white of his shirt. He wore a dark suit that made him look lean and deadly. Sexy. We looked sexy together. A sexy dangerous couple having a drink with another sexy dangerous couple.

No big deal. Nothing to see here, folks.

My heart was going like mad, though.

"I don't like this, Poppy."

"You've said that a million times. But marriage made us safe, remember?"

"Morelli's aren't known to kill other Morelli's, but anything could happen."

"Why would he want to hurt me?"

"Because I shot him not too long ago. The war between him and Caroline."

I turned on him, mouth agape. "You're just telling me this now?"

He shrugged, silent. The arm behind my head an iron bar of tension.

I no longer felt like part of a sexy dangerous couple, meeting a sexy dangerous couple for drinks. I felt like a rabbit putting its head in a trap.

✧ ✧ ✧

Ronan

THERE WAS AN ornate and imposing door. It swung open before we knock, revealing an older gentleman in a suit. A butler? A security guard? Probably both. Leo Morelli would need that.

With a low murmur, he led us deep into the castle.

A large library with white shelves that reached to the ceiling. Plush chairs formed reading nooks around the parquet floor. Windows overlooked a forest. It would have been a welcoming room if not for the occasion. Leo stood beside a tall armchair, where Haley sat.

The last time I saw her she'd been fighting for Leo's life. Right before I put a bullet in his chest. I shook off the memory, but the deep tension in my gut went nowhere. I was unarmed and Poppy was wearing that fucking dress and I'd never been more scared.

"Poppy," I wanted to stop her. To try and keep her here, so whatever revenge scheme Leo had planned it would just involve me. And that I could spare her what I'd been unable to spare Haley—watching her lover get shot.

"It will be all right," the butler / security guard murmured.

It wasn't in me to trust this person. To trust

this house. To trust anyone, outside of Poppy. But I didn't have a choice. Poppy and I crossed the library.

"Ronan," Leo said.

"Listen, if this is some kind of revenge, let Poppy go—"

"It's not," he said.

"I put a bullet in you."

"But you didn't kill me." Leo smiled at me, a dangerous man. "And I think you could have, if you wanted to. Caroline gave you orders to kill me."

"You're letting this go on a technicality?" I asked.

Haley narrowed her eyes. "I'm not letting anything go. If it were up to me, you could rot in hell for shooting Leo. But he has a soft spot for family."

Family. That was what the couple in front of me could have been, in another world. There was a sense of loss in my chest. Loss for something I've never had. "If it means anything, I'm sorry."

Leo put a hand on Haley's shoulder, as if to reassure her.

"Come on," he said. "Let's have a drink." I followed him across the room to a small drinks cart. "Irish whiskey?" he asked, lifting a decanter.

I nodded and he walked back over to me with two fingers in a crystal glass. I glanced back to see Poppy saying something to Haley. At least Haley doesn't look ready to pounce on her.

"I just did this same thing with your father," I said, gesturing toward the drinks.

"He offered you a job."

"I wouldn't call it offered."

The corner of his lip rose in answer. He seemed…lighter than he had before. Back in the days of his war with Caroline. When he was hungry for revenge. I looked over at the women. Haley pointed at something on a shelf. Poppy looked awestruck. Bonding over a library. Two sources of light in a dark room.

"You're not going to take it?" he asked.

I bit back the answer, unwilling to give him anything to use against me.

"Why am I here, Leo? If you're not going to get revenge?" I asked. "For shooting you. For putting Haley through everything?"

Leo shook his head and sat down in front of an empty fireplace. He was careful sitting back. I wondered if he still felt pain from the gunshot wound all these months later. "Sit," Leo said. "I swear you're safe."

I sat, sipping my whiskey which was excellent

and waited for Leo to get to the point.

"I should probably beat the shit out of you. Not so much for shooting me, but Haley had nightmares."

"I'm sorry," I said. And I was. That life... those things I did. The comfort I gave myself by believing in monsters and then putting them down. It didn't hold up in this room. With the pretty women talking about books and Leo Morelli having a drink with me.

Leo waved his hand, washing away the past, just like that.

I could feel Poppy's attention from across the room.

"I wouldn't wish being a Morelli bastard on anyone, but there are upsides."

"I don't need your fucking money."

"I'm not giving you a dime. I'm offering you a job. A place."

"What?"

"You think you're the first person to be in this situation? A Morelli in blood, but not name? Alone in the world?"

"Yes." Because I had felt alone for so long.

"You're not. And we take care of our own."

"You mean *you* take care of them." I'd heard the rumors about Leo taking care of Bryant's bastards, but I never thought I'd be one of them.

"You won't be working for my father or even for Lucian. I have my own business. My own interests. I have my own things I need done." His eyes flickered over to Haley and Poppy who were picking books out of shelves. "The Morelli family name can be a curse. But you can make it worth something."

"I've been a Morelli for ten minutes. I'm not that invested."

"You've been a Morelli your whole life. And you can run from it."

I smirked into my glass of whiskey.

"Or you can fight it. I don't recommend that option. The world isn't a safe place for people on their own. I think you learned that the hard way. But you can find a place here. A place where you belong."

"By working with you?"

"Get to know your family."

I sucked in a breath and finished my whiskey. "That's never really worked out for me," I said. "Family."

"No?" Leo asked, his eyes across the room on the girls. "Though, I suppose I understand."

Haley reached up for a book, revealing a bump beneath her dress. Was she pregnant?

I'd forgotten…or if not forgotten, pushed it to the back of my mind, where it had attached itself to all sorts of feelings. And not all of them were fear.

Poppy might have been pregnant, too.

"What's the job?" I asked. "Security?" I did security for Caroline. Bryant wanted me to do security for him, too. I knew what that job entailed. It might look like guns hidden in suits to most people, but the darker side had eaten my soul. Fixing. Murder.

Leo shook his head. "I work in real estate. You've done enough destruction. Try building something." He quirked his lips. "It's actually satisfying."

Building something. That does sound satisfying.

He stood and poured us another drink. "It will give you a chance to meet your cousins," he said.

"Cousins." I said it like it was a foreign word.

"Not all of us are bad."

"Haley is a Constantine," I said. "How does that work?"

A ghost of a smile. "It's simple, actually. I don't give a fuck about her parents. Or mine. We're building a life together. That's all that matters."

I got to my feet and made my way across the big room to Poppy, who greeted me with a smile. Her hand outstretched towards mine.

She might be pregnant. This moment. The start of something brand new. Our family.

I took her hand. A life line in an unexpected sea.

✧   ✧   ✧

"THAT WAS NICE," Poppy said, her head against my shoulder in the back of the car. "Wasn't it? Like not scary nice, but actually nice."

I didn't answer her and she didn't seem to need me to answer her.

"I liked Haley. A lot." It was good to see her happy. Smiling. Easy. I took a deep breath and let it out slowly. "She invited us to dinner next week. I said we'd have to see if we were free. Which, you know, is hilarious."

I didn't laugh at all her charm and she stroked my arm.

"What's wrong?" she asked.

"He offered me a job."

"Do you want a job?"

"No. And I don't need one." I had money saved up over the years. Accounts in Ireland that were doubling every year thanks to Niamh. I looked out the window at the dark sky. There were stars out here in Bishop's Landing. Lots of them tonight.

"He kept talking about family. About... how I could run from being Morelli. I could fight it or I could make something out of it."

She made a sound in her throat, her body pressed to mine. "I have cousins," I said. Apropos of nothing. "I've never had those before. I've never had...any of this before." I looked at her, her sunny face. "You only had one glass of champagne."

"Noticed that, did you?"

I didn't have the bravery to ask. Maybe I didn't want to know. I wasn't sure, but we left it there. In the quiet between us.

"Caroline's kids were like cousins to me and Zilla."

"Yeah?"

"Truthfully, it was nice. I miss how nice it was. I always wanted a big family. Big holidays. Lots of noise. Lots of kids."

Of course she did and I'd never thought about it. Not once. But in this moment I could see the appeal.

We were passing her old house. It was dark,

none of the external lights on.

"Can we stop?" She asked.

"Why?"

"There's something… I want to see if it's still there."

"Raj," I said. "Stop the car."

Poppy

I EXPECTED A burnt-out shell, broken windows and all my dresses strewn across the lawn. But it looked much the same as the night we left it. There was yellow caution tape across the front door and the windows were all dark. The lawn care service had even been by—there was one of those little signs at the edge of the lawn.

"You all right?" Ronan asked.

Parsing through all my feelings, I came up rather empty. "Yeah," I said. "I feel…nothing for this house." For the two years I'd lived terrified within its walls. "Nothing."

We got out of the car and Ronan snapped the tape in front of the door and we walked right in through the unlocked door. I turned on the lights to reveal absolute chaos. Cushions destroyed, paintings torn off the walls and ripped apart. Every drawer on the main floor had been emptied. The overhead light fixtures in the kitchen had been destroyed, leaving only bare bulbs to illuminate the minefield of cutlery on the floor.

"It's all ruined," I said. This whole life. The person I'd been. It was a stranger's house. A stranger's life.

I walked upstairs to my old bedroom. My dresses, thousands and thousands of dollars' worth of them, destroyed. My underwear and toiletries thrown around the room like confetti.

"Can you help me?" I asked, turning the light on in my closet. "I can't reach—"

He was beside me immediately.

"The very back of the top shelf. It's a small box…"

He stood on his tiptoes and felt around.

"I don't think it's there, lass," he said and the hopes I didn't want to have crashed to the ground.

"Wait," he said and managed to reach a nothing-special shoebox. But it was the most special thing I had. So special, my sister wouldn't have known about it. So special to protect myself I had to forget it even existed.

He handed it to me and I walked back out to the bedroom to set it on the mattress that had been ripped apart.

"I haven't looked in here in a long time." I took a deep breath, bracing myself for the memories and then lifted the lid.

There was a pink and blue baby blanket that Zilla had been wrapped in when she came home from the hospital as a newborn. There was a book my mother had made for me when I was little. Crinkly pages of buttons and zippers so I could practice fine motor skills. A silver rattle that had been my father's as an infant. Onesies with little elephants on them and striped footie pajamas I'd bought the first time I'd been pregnant. An ultrasound of a baby that didn't survive.

I put the lid on the box and faced him. I knew he could see my heart. How much I loved him. "Thank you."

His face was haunted. "Are you—" He gestured helplessly at my belly.

"It's too soon to tell," I said. "But if I am… I wanted these things."

"Aye." He nodded, solemn and serious.

"You'll be a good father, Ronan."

He turned his head away like I'd slapped him.

"Our baby won't care about what you used to do to survive. Our baby won't care about the blood in your veins."

"Our baby will have the same blood," he said, like it was a warning.

"You'll be a good father. You'll make your mother proud."

His breath was shattered and I wrapped my arms around him.

"Well, well," a cold voice behind us said. "The Bulldog and his bride."

CHAPTER SIXTEEN
Ronan

IN A HEARTBEAT I had my gun in my hand and Poppy behind me, but I was too late. There were three men in the bedroom with us. All of them were armed, blocking the doorway. We were trapped. Caught.

"We saw your lights on." The man in the very back, stepped forward. "Hope you don't mind."

Tiernan Morelli. Dark hair. Handsome. Smug.

Evil.

I'd been so caught up in Poppy, in the baby things and dreams that could never come true, I didn't even hear them coming. Niamh was right. This was what having a weakness did to a man like me—it put everyone around me in danger.

"Drop it," Tiernan said, pointing his gun at Poppy. "Or I'll put a bullet in her shoulder for real."

"There's no need for this," I said, putting my

gun down on the bed.

"That's not the way Bryant sees it. My dad is a little pissed with you, cousin."

"You can't kill him," Poppy said to the men, trying like a daft fucking girl to get in front of me. To protect me with her body. "He's a Morelli."

I put her behind me. Too rough. But it was rough or nothing. I thought of Niamh and her little boy with his sleeves rolled up. I stepped towards the men. "I'll come with you. Let her go."

One of Tiernan's thugs stepped forward as if to grab Poppy and I met him with my fist. Putting him on the ground. Another one swung towards me and I grabbed the gun out of the man's hand so fast he didn't have time to react.

And then I kicked him in the stomach, sending him backwards against the wall. He fell onto his hands and knees and then to the ground, gasping for breath with at least one broken rib and a diaphragm that wasn't working the way it should.

I pointed the gun at Tiernan, but I was too late. He had Poppy against his chest, the gun in his hand pressed to her head.

"You're too fucking predictable, Ronan," he said. He spread his hand out wide across her stomach, trying to get me to do something stupid.

"Stop," Poppy said, shoving his hand away. My brave fierce girl. "We'll go. No problems."

"See?" Tiernan said. "That wasn't so hard. She'll drive with me and you can follow behind. Anyone does anything stupid and she'll pay the price."

✧   ✧   ✧

Poppy

"I HEARD YOU were a meek little thing." Tiernan sat next to me with his gun on his knee as we drove from the Constantine part of Bishop's Landing to the Morelli side. "That you wouldn't be a problem."

"I always heard you were a bully and a sadist."

"Is that any way to talk to family?"

"You're no family of mine."

We crested the top of a small hill, and the Morelli mansion came into view. It was giant and medieval looking, made more sinister in the moonlight. My bravado withered a little and I pressed my hands together in my lap.

"What does Bryant want?" I asked.

"For everyone to follow his orders."

I remembered who I was before Ronan killed the senator and unlocked me from my prison. I'd been grateful and submissive. Confused and easily led. I gave away every bit of my power thinking it would keep me safe. Now, I had to be smarter. More cunning. More ruthless. I didn't have the money but I had the account numbers. It had to buy us some time. It had to buy me Ronan's life if it came to that.

The car stopped in front of the house, and I opened the door before anyone could do it for me. Ronan's car was behind us and he was getting out of his car, too. "Ronan!" I cried and he turned, and stumbled, his hands tied behind his back. The collar of his shirt wrinkled and torn. His face…

"What the fuck!" I screamed and wrapped my arms around him like armor. The two men he'd been traveling with crawled out of the car after him, each of them looking a little rough. Ronan, it seemed, had gotten a few punches in before his hands were bound behind his back.

"It was a bumpy ride," said one of the assholes as he braced a hand against his rib.

"I'm fine, Poppy," Ronan said through a split lip. His eye was swollen and there was a gash on his cheek, covering his face with blood. All my brave words in the car crumbled and I wanted to be the mouse I'd been, promising anything to keep him safe.

Except it never worked that way.

We were shuffled out of the night into the foyer, and I blinked, trying to get my eyes to adjust. I glanced over my shoulder to make sure Ronan was there and he was. Walking, chin up, battered face lifted.

I thought of Pikey Tom and what Ronan had learned from the priests. *We owe them nothing. We give them nothing.* Right. I lifted my chin and pulled my elbow from Tiernan's hand.

"I'm not a dog," I said to him. "You don't need to pull me."

He chuckled in his throat, pushed open a door and shoved me into an office. Moonlight poured through a window and settled like poured silver over Bryant Morelli.

I watched him, breathing through my panic. Ronan was pushed into the room beside me, his hands still tied behind his back.

"Well, it seems Ronan put up a fight," Bryant said as he walked around the desk to the comfortable leather chairs in front of it. A fireplace was to my left. Bookshelves to my right. There was only the door at my back. No other way out of the room that I could see unless I went running through that window. We were on the second floor.

"I'm Bryant Morelli," he said, approaching me, with his hand out, like we were at a cocktail party. "We haven't officially met."

I stood there, shaking with rage. But I looked at his hand and then back at his face. There'd be no pleasantries while Ronan was tied up. He dropped his hand. His eyes narrowed and I felt a chill down my spine.

"I thought the senator taught you better manners than that," he said.

"Untie Ronan and then we can show off our manners," I said.

Bryant shook his head. "He's the most dangerous man in the room. Only a fool would let him go. And I am no fool."

"Why don't we cut to the chase," I said, and out of nowhere, Bryant backhanded me across the face.

"You are not in charge here!"

I stumbled backwards and Ronan roared, lunging for Bryant with his hands still tied behind his back but Tiernan and the other two men were on him. Ronan fought, but Tiernan kicked his knee, sending his leg out from under him and he fell down hard on his other knee. I swallowed my scream and stared at Bryant.

"Three men against one? You really are scared

of him."

"I'm not scared of anything, Poppy. It's one of the pleasures that comes from being the apex predator." He leaned back against his desk. "What I am, is angry. I gave you a chance, Ronan. An opportunity to be a part of a dynasty. To become a king. And now… you're taking meetings with Leo?"

"We just had drinks," I said.

"Stupid girl, drinks are meetings. Dinner is meetings. Golf is meetings. When you're wealthier than God, business happens all the time. In fact," Bryant held out his hands. "This is a meeting. Why are you meeting Leo?"

I didn't say anything. I didn't know what to say. It had just been drinks. Some good brie. A surprising amount of laughing. Ronan was silent, too.

Bryant lifted a finger and Tiernan smiled with malice and punched Ronan across the face.

"Stop!" I screamed. "Stop! I'm telling the truth. It was just drinks."

"He offered you a job?" Bryant asked Ronan and after a second Ronan nodded.

"Did you take it?" Bryant asked.

"I'm not working for the Morellis," Ronan said and then spit blood on the carpet.

"You are a fucking Morelli!" Bryant shouted. "It's your blood, Ronan. It's your goddamn destiny and I don't know what I need to do to convince you." His face lit up. "Well, now, perhaps I do."

He walked over to me and I could feel the violence coming off of him in waves. The pleasure he was taking in this game.

"Touch her and I will kill you," Ronan threatened. "Lay one finger—"

Bryant touched my face. The shoulder bared by the dress and I felt my skin crawl. "I paid your husband a lot of money over the years to work for me. And he died before he could give me what he owed me."

"What does he owe you?"

"Information. Influence," he smiled at me and then grabbed me by the hair. "Perhaps I can take it out in trade."

"I'll work for you," Ronan said. "I'll take the job. Don't touch her."

Bryant's face lit up and he stepped away from me. My breath heaved in my chest.

"When?" Bryant asked.

"I need…just give me a week," Ronan panted.

"Two days. That's what I give you. Two days and you're back here where you belong. A

Morelli. Say it."

Ronan, beaten and bloody, nodded. The soul he'd been showing me. The heart. The dreams. The man he'd been, were all gone. He was the killer I met years ago. Distant. Cold and remote.

"Say it!" Bryant roared.

"A Morelli," Ronan said.

"I'll raise you up at my side like my sons, Ronan. You'll see. You'll have more power than you've ever dreamt of."

"Ronan," I whispered. "No. Don't do this."

"It's already done," Bryant said.

He gestured to the men standing behind Ronan, they stopped pressing on his shoulders and he got to his feet.

"Two days." He grinned, wolfish and confident. "Welcome to the family."

CHAPTER SEVENTEEN

Poppy

"YOUR FACE," I said once we were back in our car. I reached for him, the bleeding from his eye and lip. He dodged my touch.

"Are you all right?" he asked. He was driving. When we were dropped back off at my house, we found Raj, unconscious in the back seat of the car. He was conscious now, but in no shape to drive.

I touched my cheek, tender from the backhand. "Fine. That was more for show than anything."

"Are you really going to work for him?"

"I don't have a choice."

"Can't we... I don't know, find what the senator was doing for him?"

"How? Where? Poppy, that's all a dead end."

"Ronan—" I felt all those dreams for us vanish like they'd been popped. It was violence and more violence. I reached out to touch him and he shifted away.

My stomach knotted with fear.

At the apartment, I went to the bankers box for no good reason but that I was desperate. Perhaps there was something we'd missed. Some treasure map.

I heard Ronan back in his bedroom thumping around with something and I pulled out the files we'd already looked through. The plastic bag of all my jewelry was still on the table and I picked it up and tossed it on the couch to get it out of the way.

Ronan came stomping into the room with a leather bag open in his hands. In the bag I saw a bunch of my new clothes all bunched up. "What are you doing?" I asked, though it was painfully obvious.

"Are you pregnant?" He asked me that question without looking at me. "Is that why we went to your house? To get that shit? And don't fucking lie to me."

I flinched at him calling that box shit.

"I…I don't know yet."

He sucked in a deep breath. "When do you know?"

"Two weeks."

"Jesus Christ, Poppy." He looked sideways, his jaw hard. He'd washed his face and changed his shirt, but he looked deadly. As deadly as I'd ever seen him. And far away.

"Don't be mad at me," I said. "Be mad at science."

"I want you out of my house. I want you out of the country."

I blinked at him and went back to the box. I should have expected this. I should have seen it coming. "No."

"I don't want you here."

Even though I knew what he was doing, it still stung. He grabbed the bag of jewelry off the table and I snagged the edge of it as he was about to put it in the suitcase.

"I'm not leaving," I said.

"Jesus, you really are pathetic. I don't love you."

The truth was, I knew that. I knew he didn't love me and maybe he'd never love me. Not in any conventional way. But we were long past conventional. But I also knew what he was doing, trying to make me safe. He tore the bag out of my hand, ripping the thin plastic. Jewelry spilled out onto the couch. A waterfall of gold and diamonds. Turquoise and sapphires. I didn't care about the jewelry; I'd throw it out the window if I had to.

"I know what you're trying to do to me," I

said. "You've been trying to do this practically since the minute we met."

"What's that?"

"Keep me safe by pushing me away. But the safest place for me in the world is with you."

"You believe that? After everything that just happened? What the hell is wrong with you, Poppy?"

"Nothing," I snapped. "So stop treating me like a fool."

"I can't keep you safe if you're here. You talk about revenge. You talk about war. This is what war looks like, Poppy. Pack your things," he said. "Leave and you're free."

"What about you?"

"I'm never free, Poppy," he yelled. "I'm a killer. That's all I am. That's all I'll ever be. I'm a fucking Morelli *and* the Constantine monster. Don't you understand, this is my world."

It wasn't just his father who made him believe he was a weapon. Or where he was raised. Or the priests and losing his friend Tommy. It was Caroline, too. No boy grew into a man believing his only worth was killing people unless that was reinforced every step.

"You killed the senator because he hurt me."

"Why do you want to make that noble?" he

cried. "What is wrong with you that you want to make that noble?"

"Because the rules are different with you," I cried. "With this world."

"And that's why you need to leave. You need the regular world, Poppy. Where good guys are good guys not because they didn't put a bullet in a man's head. Where fairy godmothers don't save you just so they can fuck up your life. Where—"

I stood. "You've ruined me for the regular world, Ronan," I told him. "The only world I want is what you and I build together. If you're staying, then I'm staying too. You want me to leave, you have to come with me."

"Why do you want this?" He honestly didn't know. Didn't see. And I would take the rest of my life convincing him if that was what he needed.

"I love you."

"Poppy—"

"I do. I love you." I would say it until he believed it. "I love you. I love—"

He dropped the bags and grabbed me, lifted me off my feet and stomped me across the room to the wall between two windows. I expected him to shake me and tell me to grow up. That he would never love me. But instead he asked in a low, heated voice, "How do you know?"

I blinked, stunned by the question, by the torment in his face. He arched his hips against me and I felt the hard length of his cock against my belly and moaned in my throat. "Because that's not love," he snarled in my face, trying to defile everything between us. "Anyone can fuck."

"No one makes me feel like you do."

"You liked Eden well enough on that plane."

"Only because you were watching."

He tried to stay so furious, he did. He clung to it with all his strength. And I almost felt bad for him. I reached up and pushed his dark hair off his face. His beautiful, broken face. His hands left my shoulders to grab on to the windowsill and I was boxed in between the window and his body.

And I didn't want to be anywhere else. I kissed his forehead. His cheek. He dropped his face against mine.

"I love you," I whispered against his face. He flinched and I said it again. And then again. Binding him to me with my hope and my heart. With everything I was sure we could be if he would believe in me. Believe in what I saw when I looked at him. He wasn't just a killer. He had a code that was pure iron. He was a victim, still grieving. Still hurting. He was my fierce protector and he would break the laws of man if I was hurt.

If I was a queen, he was my king. And we'd find our own fucking kingdom.

"I love you," I said again, determined to say it until he believed me.

"How do you know?" he asked.

I cupped his face and lifted it so our eyes met. "How do I know I love you?" I read the question in his eyes. And I realized this wasn't his searching for a compliment. He honestly didn't know how this was supposed to feel and, granted, I hadn't had a lot of experience, but I'd loved people in my life. But he'd had no one. Everyone who should have loved him left him. Or used him. Twisted him into this man who thought the only way for him to live was alone. A version of himself he never should have been.

"Because I want to make you happy," I said. "Because you make me happy."

"How? By fucking you?" Again, he wasn't even trying to be crude. These were the metrics he was used to in his life. "Killing for you?"

"Because I know sometimes what you're thinking. Because you know what I'm thinking. Because when you smile at me, I feel like I've won something."

He dropped his head back down against mine, grinding our foreheads together. "I'm no prize,

Poppy."

"You're my prize," I said.

"Fuck, you deserve so much more than this. Where's your fucking pride, lass?" I could feel how he was fighting this. Fighting me. All the strength of a last-ditch effort.

"Who gives a shit about pride?" I asked. "What has pride ever gotten me? You make me feel like a queen. Like anything is possible. After years of being hurt and scared and never ever being able to put what I want first, you are what I get. A man who takes me to the end of the earth to be safe. Who opens up all his wounds to show me his pain. A man who makes me omelets and farl and when he touches me my whole world changes."

I put my fingers through his hair. Ran them down over his neck and shoulders.

"And I think, Ronan Byrne, you're only getting started. If you let yourself love me…" I whistled, tears burning in my eyes as I imagined the fierceness he would bring to loving me. I gasped, thinking of the baby I might be carrying. And the way Ronan would love it. "We'd be a force of nature. We'd be untamed."

Something in my words kicked something over inside of him and his hands left the windowsill to tear and pull at my clothes. His mouth found mine and it was not so much a kiss as it was a storm. "How do you know?" he asked again, still not ready to believe me.

"Because I know."

He was wild and fierce and I matched him. Desperate for the way I felt when he touched me and when I touched him. He got the zipper on my dress half undone and tore the rest of it off. I stood there in underwear and nothing else, visible to anyone who looked up, and I didn't care. As long as he was touching me. My fingers got his belt loose, the zipper of his pants, but he knocked my hands away and fell to his knees in front of me.

"You destroy me, Poppy. You fucking ruin me. Who the fuck do you think you are to be so brave? To be so fierce?"

"I am what you've made me," I said, stroking his hair back from his face.

He put his mouth on me through the satin of my underwear. And my hands flew back, my ugly ring smacking against the glass hard enough to break it, but he didn't move. Could not be distracted. He licked me through the satin, over and over again until I was out of my mind with it.

"What do you want, Poppy?" he whispered

against me. I wanted him to love me. To love me like I loved him. And I had to believe I was right, but I couldn't force him. I couldn't make him feel something when he wasn't ready. And maybe…maybe he'd never be ready. That was a risk I knew in my heart was true. That I might be alone in my feelings for him for the rest of my life.

"More," I said, and he chuckled low in his throat. I could feel a kind of relief roll off of him, because this he could give me. This cost him nothing. He would give me more until there was nothing left of him. He eased my panties over my shoes, leaving them on. He ran his hands slowly up my legs. The outside of my calves. My knees. My thighs. I was panting, unable to catch my breath. My entire world narrowed to his touch on my skin. Nothing mattered outside of this.

I only cared about Ronan. "You're so pretty," he whispered, his hands easing from my hips, across my belly to the ache between my legs. His thumbs stroked me, slid me open. Held me open. "So pink, Poppy. You're so pink and wet."

He kissed me, and if he was kissing any other part of my body, it would be chaste. Reverent. "Ronan," I groaned. My hand clutching his hair, pushing him against me.

He resisted, the asshole, just to torment me.

"More?"

"Please."

And he gave it to me. He pushed me against the wall and held me there, his mouth between my legs. He shouldered my thighs out wider and cupped my hips, holding me still. Holding me down. I was wet and he was loud and there was no room for shame or embarrassment. "Fuck," he kept saying against my flesh. "Fuck, Poppy."

He sucked on my clit, slid a finger inside of my body, and I moaned high in my throat, my hips searching for the right pressure, the right angle, trying as best I could to have more. To get more of him.

"Fuck, yes," he said, and I looked down to find him looking up at me, his mouth wet, his body at my feet. His hand was buried between my legs. And maybe there was a disconnect for him between the word *love* and what he felt for me, but I saw it in his eyes as he watched me fucking myself against his fingers. Naked against a window, spread open and so mad for him I didn't care about anything but him. But us. This is how I know, I thought. Because you are what matters most to me.

And he looked at me the same way.

"Yes," I moaned, my fingers in his soft hair.

He put his mouth back on me, messy and wild, and I exploded in orgasm. I lost myself in it. In him. My brain was empty, my body full of starlight. I was made of pleasure, and when my legs buckled, he caught me. I put my mouth to his, catching my breath by taking his. And of course, he gave it to me. He would give me anything. Everything. *That's how I know.*

"Please," I whispered, my hand finding the hard length of his cock. I gripped him in my fist until he bit my name out through his teeth. I needed more. I needed everything. And I needed it until I couldn't take any more.

That's how I know. He stood up, my strong gorgeous Ronan, swinging me into his arms.

"Ronan, you're hurt—"

"Not enough to stop."

His mouth was on mine as he walked us into the back bedroom with its giant bed and soft sheets. He laid me down in the middle of it and I pulled off his shirt. His skin was soft and warm and I traced the muscles of his back as he flexed, lifting himself onto one hand, magically getting rid of the last of his clothes. He took care of everything, this man. Sandwiched between him and the bed, I eased down as best I could, kissing his chest. His hard nipple. The soft hair down the center of his belly. For such a hard man, he really was so soft.

"Poppy," he groaned, shifting away from me. "Ya can't."

"Well, we both know that's not true." I kissed his chin. The skin beneath it—also soft. The edge of his ear.

"I want to fuck you, lass," he said in my ear, making goose bumps ripple over my skin. Over my heart. I spread my legs, letting him between my thighs. The hard length of his cock fell against my wet pussy and we both groaned and shook. I slipped my fingers around him, pressing him harder against me, lifting my hips higher until I felt the head of his cock at the entrance of my body. He kissed me again and again. Hard kisses. Clumsy. His nose bumped mine. His teeth cut the edge of my lip and I realized he was barely in control.

Ronan. My Ronan, who had spent every moment we were together under almost perfect control was *losing it*. Never in my life had I felt so gorgeous, so *loved*. Sweating, with my own come slick on my thighs. This terrible haircut and undoubtedly raccoon eyes. He was shaking with desire for me. "You make a mess of me, Poppy. The second I'm inside you, it's going to be all over."

"Ronan," I groaned, dying for him. For this version of him. I pressed him against me again, arching my hips so he hit my clit and got messy with my come. Our breathing was ragged and I could feel him shaking. "I love you, Ronan," I said, smiling into his harsh beloved face. "I dream of having your babies—"

He shifted me, pulled me, and in a breath was so deep inside me I screamed. He stopped again. His hands cradling my face. "*A chuisle*, I'm sorry. I'm—"

"Good," I gasped, though it stung deep inside and I felt like I'd been impaled to the bed. But from one heartbeat to the next, the sting eased and I was just so full. Stretched and full. Of him.

"It's so good," I said, stroking his face. Tears burned in my eyes, not from the pain of loving Ronan. Always from the pleasure. I arched against him and he pressed his head to my neck and eased himself out of my body. I shook and shuddered against him. I could feel the tremors in his body. The muscles of his back. His arms where he was braced by my shoulders.

So much control. In every situation. So much so he never let himself bein fear of losing that control. In fear of pain. That he was hanging by a thread with me felt miraculous. Felt like a gift.

"I love you," I whispered in his ear, and he flinched, almost like he wanted to get away from me. But I wrapped my legs around his waist, changing the angle, and when he slid back inside me, he was deeper than I could even dream. "I love you," I said on a choked sob because it was unbearably true. "I love you so much."

He fucked me across the bed, three massive strokes, and then he held on to me so hard it pulled my hair. "Poppy," he groaned and then another thrust and he roared it, my name bouncing around the dark room as he came inside of me, shaking and whispering nonsense I could not understand. I was limp and loose, though there was an orgasm waiting inside of me, humming between my legs.

He eased out of me and I moaned, still sensitive, still needing him. Between my legs I could feel the slip-slide of his come and I pressed my thighs together, gasping at the sparks that set off. "Are you all right, Poppy?" he whispered, wiping the tears from my cheeks. The sweat from my breasts. "Did I hurt you, *a chuisle*?"

"No," I sighed. "You didn't hurt me, Ronan."

I stroked his face, lifted my face to kiss him. And then again. The taste of him impossible to get enough of. I could kiss him forever. Hungrier and hungrier for him. "Ah, fuck, lass," he said. "You need more."

CHAPTER EIGHTEEN

H E ROLLED ONTO his side and turned me so my back was against him. His arms wrapped around me, and I felt small and cradled and safe against his chest. I pressed my ass against his dick, growing harder against me. I reached for him, the fever in my blood getting hotter and hotter. He chuckled against my neck, his breath against my skin, and I shivered and whimpered. I reached my hand back, hungry for him. So hungry it felt like I was empty.

"You need this, Poppy." His fingers ran from my stomach to between my legs. He groaned when he touched me.

"I need you," I whispered. "Please, Ronan. I need—"

He shifted me, arranged me the way he wanted and slid back inside of me. He was hard and I was hot and together we were wet and it all felt electric. We were electric. We were fire. We were something elemental. Like air and earth. This feeling was timeless.

We were endless. He fucked me sweet and slow, his fingers pressed hard against my clit. "More," I whispered, clutching at his hands, pressing him harder against me.

"No."

"Ronan," I snapped.

"Trust me," he said, and then again, kissing my temple. Sweet. So sweet, it hurt. "Trust me."

I let go of his hands, relaxed myself against him, let myself be touched and used and stroked. It was slow and long and a pace that made me want to crawl out of my skin and I was sobbing his name, desperate and wild, the orgasm curling and twisting inside of my body. I'd reach for it and it would slip out of my fingers. "Please," I begged. Again and again.

"Are you ready?"

"Yes. Anything."

He pulled out of me, and when I growled, he only laughed. "I like you like this," he said. "It makes me want to keep you in bed and never let you go."

He rolled me onto my stomach and grabbed one of the pillows that I hadn't knocked to the floor and shoved it under my hips. He moaned, running his hands up and over my ass, and I knew what was coming. The way he'd been getting me ready for this since the cottage. "You give me so much," he said. "Every time you surrender. You're so strong, Poppy."

He used his fingers to scoop up the come, mine and his, that was dripping from my body. He smeared it against my asshole, slowly working in a finger. I panted and moaned. The pain of it was fleeting, and when it left, it left behind an unbearable ache. A profound emptiness. He worked in another finger and I kept making a high keening sound in my throat as he rolled over me, pressed my legs out wide.

"I don't want to hurt you, lass."

"Then don't stop. Please don't ever stop."

Slowly, gently, he pushed himself inside of me, and every time I asked him to stop, he did. And he kissed my cheek and told me how beautiful I was. How perfect. And it took a thousand years and no time at all until he whispered,

"There, Poppy. You've taken all of me."

And still, somehow, I said, "More."

He growled in his throat, my favorite sound. The sound of him coming untamed. "You'll be the fucking end of me, Poppy."

And then he was fucking me. One hand under my body, his fingers against my clit. I was starlight and magic. My body completely unfamiliar to me. Brand new. The way he stroked me and held me, it went on and on until I had to twitch away from him. His cock and his fingers. His warmth and the sound of his voice. All of it too much. My body was raw and he was too much.

"Ronan," I cried, suddenly scared.

"I got you, lass. I've got you. You're safe." And it was the truest thing I knew. The best thing in my life. This man would keep me safe.

I exploded in orgasm, my whole soul pulled into it. I felt him behind me, stiffen and then swear, holding still as I clamped down on his cock and couldn't stop. The orgasm kept going, my body buzzing and without boundaries.

I was boneless and limp underneath him and he grabbed my hips, holding me the way he wanted and used me for his own pleasure. Used me until he came, shouting my name and gripping my hips hard enough I'd have bruises tomorrow. But the pain didn't begin to register now. I was only pleasure. I was endless light.

As slowly as he entered me, he withdrew, hissing and whispering my name. I wanted to tell him I was all right. That nothing in my life had ever felt so good, but my body didn't work.

Slowly, he turned me in his arms, my body wet and sticky against his. His hair was slick against his face and I longed to push it back, out of his pretty blue eyes, but if I had hands, they were broken. I love you. I love you so much it hurts.

"You okay?" he asked, kissing my cheek. My lips. My other cheek. He brushed my hair off my face with the flat of his hand.

"I've never…" There were twenty things I could say. I've never come that hard. I've never had sex that good. Been fucked so well. "Felt this way."

"Me neither," he said, surprising me.

I put my hands over his, pressing him against my stomach.

I rolled to face him. A slice of shadowy light seeped out from the blinds on the window and highlighted his face. The eye and the slice on his cheek. I touched the bruising as gently as I could. "I don't want…" I stopped, unsure of how to say this.

"What?"

I picked up his hand, the one with the scar on his wrist from the downspout when he had to jump through a window. "I don't want our child to jump out a window because something bad was coming through their door."

"No," he whispered. "Me, neither."

He was silent for a long time, his eyelids drifted shut and he forced them back open through a force of will.

"When's the last time you slept?" I asked him.

"I sleep," he lied. He was so tired he sounded drunk.

"You didn't sleep at the cottage. You didn't sleep last night."

I stroked his face, and with every touch of my fingertips, his eyes half shut. A spike of sweetness went right through me. "We're safe here," I said. "No one can hurt you here."

"You think I don't sleep because I'm worried about myself?" No. I didn't think that. "I don't sleep, Poppy, because of you. I'm worried about you. And Bryant…the deadline."

"I'm safe," I whispered. "We have two days. You've made me safe. Sleep." I smiled into his face. "I'll keep you safe."

He was so tired he didn't even react. He was so tired he was asleep before his eyes even shut. His breathing soft and even, his body relaxed and heavy against mine. I curled my arms around him and held him the way he never let me hold him when he was awake. With my arms around his shoulders, his head against mine. His knees curled up against my legs. Ronan was so strong. The strongest man I knew. He was determined and stubborn. He was brave. But he was also human and I loved him more the more of his humanity he showed me. And this, right now, I loved him so much it brought me to tears.

But then I had to go pee.

Carefully, so I didn't wake him, I rolled away from him. Though it was obvious he was out, like out out. Ronan was nearly superhuman, but there was a limit to how much a human body could endure. And he'd hit the wall. I put on a robe and made some coffee with Ronan's fancy coffee maker before texting my sister to see how she was doing.

Fine, she texted back right away.

How are things with Jacob?

The little dots on her end appeared and then disappeared. I waited for her text to arrive but then the dots showed up again. Disappeared. Reappeared.

I called her.

"What's going on?" I asked when she picked up. "I don't..." she whispered, and I could hear some scuffling on her end, the creak of her old wood floors. "Zilla?"

"I don't really know," she finally said in a

slightly louder voice.

"Are you safe? Is he—"

"He kissed me last night. Or…I kissed him. It's blurry."

My eyes opened wide and I was stunned into silence. Zilla, for all her unpredictability, was pretty predictable when it came to men. She had one very limited use for them, and otherwise she stayed away. "He's sleeping now. Like really sleeping. The guy is pretty fucking tired."

"That's weird. So is Ronan," I said, walking into the living room where my bag and all my jewelry was spread across the couch. The clothes I'd been wearing were in a pile in front of the window. The bag Ronan had been packing for me was forgotten on the floor. God, the plane and now having sex against this window.

Being Mrs. Ronan Byrne was turning me into someone new. I liked her. She was ballsy and sexy and owned all of that. It still felt a little bit like I was pretending, but I imagined change didn't happen overnight. I needed to remember that when it came to Ronan, too. He could not change simply because I wanted him to. And it seemed, a little, like he wanted to, too.

"He's…" Zilla sighed. "He's a nice guy. And he…gets me. Like I don't have to hide anything from him. I don't have to pretend."

I realized in her voice that pretending must be a large part of her life and I ached for her the way I always did. And I was proud of her and how strong she was. "That's amazing, Zilla."

"He's still scary as fuck, but it's not hard hanging out with him. He laughs at my jokes."

"Good," I said, and started picking my shit up off the floor.

"How are you and Ronan?"

I laughed because that was some kind of complicated. "Good," I finally said, choosing not to go into the war we were wading into. "I think. I mean, I think he's coming around to the idea of us. That he can believe me when I tell him I love him."

I didn't tell her about Ronan working for Bryant.

"Why do you do that?" she whispered.

"Do what?"

"Love someone who has no way of loving you back. Why do you give so much of yourself away when there's no return?"

Another sunrise through the windows. My whole world was upside down here. I slept during the day and was held at gunpoint at night. And through it all there was Ronan. Ronan holding me tight. Keeping me safe. Loving me when he didn't know the word.

"I think he can love me back. I think he does. But I can love him enough for both of us until he feels what I feel."

"What if…what if some people aren't made to feel love, Poppy? Or what if it's been taken out of them? What if…"

I heard the question she was really asking and it broke my heart.

"I don't think it's love that gets taken out of someone. I think it's trust. Some people have been hurt so badly the only way to get better was to only trust themselves." I thought of Ronan and Caroline. I thought of Ronan's mother.

"I love you, Zilla," I said. "I hope you find some happiness with your murder accountant."

"And I hope you find some with Ronan."

Me too. I couldn't tell her how fragile my happiness was. How loving Ronan felt like an act of recklessness and at the same time the safest thing I'd ever done. Maybe, I realized, that's what love was.

It was being terrified of the leap but being sure of being caught.

We hung up and I tossed my phone on the couch and then bent down to pick up the plastic bag with its guts of gemstones.

I picked up the necklaces and set them on the coffee table. My foot nudged the jeweler's case for Jim's pearls and I reached down and grabbed it by the lid. These fucking things. Jim said they were heirlooms, a gift from his grandfather to his grandmother and passed down to his mother and then to me. Every time I wore them, he made it clear that I was somehow a disappointment to him, unable to live up to his mother's memory. She'd apparently been a strong woman, stronger, he thought, than me, because I allowed him to break my finger and punch me in the stomach.

I hated these pearls. They were chains to the past. And ugly as fuck.

I picked it up by the lid but the ancient clasp on it was unpredictable and opened, while the box was upside down and the pearls with the velvet insert the pearls rested on fell out. And with them a small chrome thumb drive.

Poppy

I LOOKED DOWN at that little thumb drive and nailed my hopes to the ground. There was no way the senator would store whatever information he was gathering for Bryant Morelli in a thumb drive hidden in my jewelry.

Ludicrous. But…still. I picked up the thumb drive. It was the kind that you twisted part of it and the USB came out. Part of me wanted to wake Ronan immediately, but he needed sleep and there could be anything stored on this thing.

Maybe he was writing a terrible spy novel.

Or he had child pornography.

Maybe it was pictures of me sleeping.

In Ronan's guest room there was a desktop computer and a laptop on the edge of the bed. The laptop was brand new and didn't have a USB port, but the desktop was older and I slipped the USB in the port. I wiggled the mouse and the screen came to life.

Password protected, of course.

He had a password on his laptop and I'd watched him type it in and I made a guess that Ronan wasn't the type to have more than one.

I typed in *StBrigid* and the computer opened up. How like Ronan to keep his pain as sharp as he could. I clicked open files.

It took a second to realize what it was. Dollar amounts paid to other senators and representatives. Bribes, I thought. I recognized some of the names. Men and women on committees and Bryant was influencing their political votes.

Which made sense and to some extent I'd expected. Not laid out like this. Lord, the senator was a stupid man.

But there were also hundreds of photographs. Audio recordings of phone calls. Video surveillance. Private jet log book entries. Bank account balances.

All of Caroline Constantine.

THE BEDROOM WAS still dark, Ronan still sleeping. He had his head buried in the pillows, the blanket down around his waist revealing the slope of his back. The tender skin under his arms. The room smelled like him, his skin and a little bit like sex.

Before Bryant put his hands on me, there'd been a chance for us. A door opening to a different kind of life. But then Bryant shut that door. And the ferry boat captain was a killer again.

Could I use this to open the window back up?

He'd saved my life. Could I save his? He would not appreciate this. At least not at first. But I knew if there was going to be a life for us. It started with this.

I wanted to be pregnant. I wanted Ronan's

baby.

I wanted Ronan to know something good and sweet about his mother. I wanted what I saw in Ronan's eyes last night.

A chance.

There'd been a whole lot of doing things Ronan's way in the short period of time we'd been together. And his way was bloody and confrontational and constantly walking a tightrope of kill or be killed. It was destroying him. Which was fine if you were a killer who didn't care about living or dying. It was another thing entirely for a man who was loved. Who would be missed. Who, if given a chance, might have a life.

A family.

I was going to do this my way. Operating on faith that it might be better. That for once I could take care of him. He wouldn't like it. At all. But I could do it.

For us, though he wouldn't see it that way. Or maybe he would after last night. I had to believe something I said made a difference to him. That in giving him every part of myself to him, he saw his own value.

If he didn't, I would do it again tonight. And the next night. I would take his pain and his doubt and I would give him back my faith. My love. My surrender would make him clean.

I went back into the other room and grabbed a piece of paper and black marker. I wrote a note for Ronan and left it quietly on my pillow. My whole life people had been calling the shots and I was always one step behind. Being led and cleaning up as I went. This was going to be different.

For Ronan, it had to be different.

I sent a message I hoped would be received in the manner it had been sent.

Outside the apartment door was Raj, who after getting knocked unconscious last night was back at his post. I wondered if Ronan saw that loyalty. If he even knew how to see it. Raj practically jumped at attention when I stepped out.

"Raj," I said. "Are you all right?"

"Nothing some aspirin couldn't fix." He rubbed at the back of his head and gave me a cheeky grin. "Did you need something?"

"A favor."

"Oh no," he said, shaking his head. "We're not doing this again. Last time I let you leave without him, I thought Ronan was going to kill me, like."

"Different kind of favor." The phone in my

hand buzzed.

An incoming message from Caroline.

I'll be there in a half hour.

"Someone's coming to the apartment, but don't bring them here. Take them up to the roof. Ronan can not know."

"I don't like this, Poppy," he said.

"I know." But that didn't change anything. I took the thumb drive and everything I'd printed off of it. Ronan's laptop and I went upstairs to wait.

To fight.

✧　✧　✧

CAROLINE WAS NOTHING if not punctual and thirty-five minutes later the door to the rooftop garden was thrown open and Caroline stepped out into the sunlight. She wore a cream dress and nude stilettos. She came dressed for battle and I was wearing yoga pants and one of Ronan's shirts.

The way we did battle was so different. I used to think power looked like her. But there were so many different versions of power. So many different versions of control.

Of love.

Family.

"The roof? Really?" she asked and wrenched

her elbow away from Raj. "I'm fine from here."

The door clanged shut behind her and it was just us in the early sunshine. Bees working their way from flower to flower.

"Your message was compelling, Poppy, I hope you weren't lying."

"No. I have information on Bryant Morelli that you're going to be interested in." I lifted the file and the thumb drive.

She held out her hands, her face set in an expression of "so?"

"Apparently Bryant Morelli was paying the Senator to keep very close tabs on you. There are photographs, video surveillance. Your phones were bugged."

"What?" She honestly looked stunned. And at this point I had enough faith in my ability to read Caroline that I believed she was telling the truth. Caroline did not know what Bryant was doing.

"For years. At least as long as we were married. Probably long before."

"That fucking weasel, it's why he approached me at that god damn luncheon. I should have known." She turned, facing the skyline, gathering her composure. "No one is what they seem, Poppy. I thought I'd learned that lesson."

For a second I felt pity for her. And then I

remembered all the ways she'd fucked with me over the years.

"How deep does the surveillance go? All the way into Halcyon? Into my family?" I heard the question she wasn't asking. Who else betrayed me?

"Honestly, Caroline, it just seemed like Bryant was interested in you. It looks like he skipped opportunities to spy on your family and on the business. He could have really done some damage. But he didn't."

Caroline blinked. Again and then again and I realized, all at once, that she seemed to be blinking back tears.

"Are you all right?" I asked her.

"I don't know why I'm surprised," Caroline said and then took a deep breath. "That man has been a part of my life for so long. For, and I'm not kidding, Poppy, as long as I can remember, my life has been tied to Bryant's. And it wasn't always a war."

I held my breath. Every part of this was unexpected. I'd gone into this ready to fight and now I was on the verge of comforting her?

"What are you saying, Caroline?"

"I'm saying he wasn't always like this. So…hard. So full of violence. He was always intense, but it wasn't so unhinged."

"Did you have a relationship with him?"

"I did. But I met Lane not too long after that..." She shrugged. "Bryant does not accept losing."

"You're saying he has spent billions of dollars to watch you. From afar?"

"It's almost romantic, isn't it?" Caroline said.

This is what passed for romance in Caroline's life? It was sad, that's what it was. I thought of Ronan downstairs and how he could turn me inside out with a touch. How I would walk to the ends of the earth to keep him safe.

No. I'd take Ronan's romance forever.

"So, why did you bring me here?" Caroline said.

I explained Bryant's demands that Ronan come and work for him and this information might be the only thing that could keep Ronan safe, but only if I returned it to him.

Caroline shook her head. "Bryant will never keep his word."

"I know," I said.

"He'll tell you you're safe and then when he wants to pull the chain—"

"I know, Caroline," I said wondering how deep their relationship went. How dangerous it had gotten. "That's why I'm giving you the file."

Caroline's eyes went wide, the grief that had clung to her on this roof vanished. "You'll give me that?" she asked.

"I want Ronan free of both of you," I said. "You're the only one who can manage Bryant." And now that I knew the origins of their relationship, I saw why she had that power. Because he gave it to her.

Obsession.

Love?

I held out the documents and she took them. Though when she pulled them I didn't let go. "I've made copies," I said. "And there's enough information in here that could damage your legacy for a long time. Fuck me on this Caroline and I will ruin you."

I let go of the files and she clutched them to her chest.

"I'll keep you safe, Poppy," Caroline said. "The way I promised your mother I would."

"Don't bring my mother into this," I said.

"Fine. I'll protect you the way I always should have."

Again, I felt that longing to believe her. To let her promise mean something to me. But that was a child's dream and Caroline had shown me her true colors enough times that I knew not to believe her. It was why I'd made copies, after all.

I'd learned my lessons from this woman.

Good and bad.

CHAPTER NINETEEN

Ronan

I COULD COUNT on my hands the number of times I'd slept a full night's sleep and almost all of them were before St. Brigid's. There were a few times, alone on the jet, traveling from Ireland to New York, I was exhausted enough to trust I was safe. I fell asleep so deep the attendants had to wake me when we landed.

But no, most of those blissful nights of sleep happened when I was a kid. Before I realized Da was leaving the house after he kicked me up to bed.

But after all that with Poppy, after letting down every guard I had left against her, I slept like a babe.

It was disorienting, waking up without fear or panic. I reached for her, expecting to find her soft and warm, her hair a tangle over her face, her body a breath away from ready for me.

But instead I hit cold air and a piece of paper.

I was well used to dread and it filled me as I blinked my eyes open and turned the paper over so I could read it.

Trust me. I love you.

I crumpled it up in my fist and hurled myself from the bed. She was gone, the daft girl. The stupid lass. The apartment was empty. The jewels tossed over the couch like they meant nothing. The bankers box spilled onto the floor where I'd shoved it.

She'd been looking through the box again. And she must have found something, otherwise why would she leave?

Trust me. I love you.

Or she'd gone to strike some new deal with either Bryant or Caroline. I held myself still against the hurricane-force fear. I clenched my fists and I tried. I did. I tried to find whatever part of myself hadn't been scoured by my life. I wanted Poppy to be right. For there to be, inside of me, what she saw.

A garden fallow and waiting but still a garden.

I could trust her.

And I could trust she loved me, and this raging, burning desire and fear I felt for her—I could trust that, too. And I could stand there and put down all my weapons. I could believe in her. In her good strength and her sound mind.

She would not hurt me. Or betray me.

But what if she's pregnant?

Walking around with my child in her belly and it wasn't her I didn't trust. It was the world. The world that would hurt her if I wasn't standing between it and her. My whole life, I realized, from one breath to the next, the only life I wanted, the only one with meaning was to be standing between her and what would hurt her.

"Poppy!" I roared. I roared it again, throwing open the door to my apartment only to find Raj.

"The fuck, Ronan?" he said. "Get some fucking pants on you."

"Have you seen Poppy? She's—"

"Upstairs. She's had a meeting—" I pushed past Raj and ran up the stairs, hitting the door onto the rooftop patio.

"Ronan?" Poppy said, smiling at me over her teacup, even though she was confused. Smiling at me because she was just so happy to see me.

Me.

And at the sight of her I was…I was complete. I'd never thought to call this feeling love. Because love, from what I'd seen, was ever-changing and mercurial. It was a thin motive and after-the-fact excuses. This feeling in my body for her, this reckoning in my soul—it was so much bigger. It was fundamental. I fell to my knees in front of her, thinking of that wedding ceremony, those ancient words I'd spoken from the whole of my chest.

"Ronan?" She looked at me, worried. "Are you all right? Did something happen?"

"You," I said. I was distantly aware that Niamh was there too, not approving of any of this, I imagined. But this girl with the eyes and the smile. This girl was all that mattered.

"You happened, Poppy."

She stroked my lips, and in her eyes I could see that she understood the power of what was happening in my chest. This silent-communication thing we had between us was working. But she deserved to hear the words. And I needed to say them.

"I'm yours, Poppy," I said to her face. All that I am. Every part of me. My violence and my bloodstained hands. Like I was a knight and she was a queen, I would defend her to my death. "I love you and I'm yours."

She set down the teacup and touched my bare shoulders, my face. She pressed her hand over my heart and I put mine over hers. "You are mine," I said to her. "You were mine the minute I saw you."

I wasn't born with poetry, or if I had, it was quickly beaten out of me, but I was fucking Irish. And in my Irish soul I knew she'd been mine forever. This life and the next until the world ended.

"I am yours and you are mine," she whispered and then smiled at me with her beautiful smile. Full of grace and wonder and strength. Poppy Byrne was just getting started and I was the luckiest man on earth to be by her side.

CHAPTER TWENTY

Ronan

W E TOOK EVERYTHING downstairs so I could put on some pants.

At my dining room table Poppy explained to me what she found.

"He's been following her?" I asked.

"More than followed. He's been…watching her. For years."

"And they had a relationship?" I tried to imagine something more terrifying than Bryant and Caroline in love, but I was hard pressed to see it.

Poppy nodded, eyes twinkling as she sipped her coffee. The girl loved gossip. "It's actually a little sad. He lost her to Lane and he never got over her."

"Or maybe he never got over losing," I said.

"I like my version better," she said with a pout.

"And all of this happened while I was sleeping?" I asked.

"Well, we're not done yet," Poppy said. "You need to talk to Bryant."

This part was difficult. I was a man who got assurances with blood. The deals I made were with violence. This… blackmail? Trusting Caroline. I didn't know how to trust it. If I could.

"Trust me," Poppy said. "I know it's hard, but trust me. This is how we get out from under Bryant."

I looked down at her face. And she saw in my hesitation something I couldn't even put a name to.

"Do you want to?" she whispered. "Do you want to be free of him?"

"I'm a Morelli, Poppy, I'll never be totally free."

She nodded. "But working for him. With him. Taking that place at his side that he seems so hell-bent on giving you? Do you want that?"

I'd been fighting so hard to get out of this cage and now that I was really about to be free, I felt fear leaving that cage.

"I don't know who I am without violence. I've been in it for too long. The blood on my hands…it's permanent, Poppy."

"I don't believe that," she said and stood. "But I can't…" Her voice broke and I hated myself for hurting her. For giving her a second of doubt.

I realized, at once, how Poppy was some combination of all the women in my life.

Loving like Sinead. Clever like Caroline. Fierce like Niamh.

"I love you," she said. "And I think you're so much more than the weapon people have made you. And I'm yours no matter what you decide but if you could see yourself the way I see you, this wouldn't even be a question. I can't make this decision for you." Poppy said and stroked my face.

She left me to do what only I could do.

I thought about Jacob saying he didn't want to kill again, but that if anyone hurt Zilla, he'd kill them. I'd understood those words the minute he said them. I didn't want to be anyone's weapon. Not anymore. But I would be her shield forever.

Did I want to stop being a weapon?

Did I want to stop fighting a war that wasn't mine?

The answer was yes. The answer was please. The answer was so complicated I didn't know how to say it out loud. I thought of Niamh and I felt guilty for finding love. For wanting a future, while she was here with her chilblains and 1970s kitchen. The way she held herself still and clung to all her mistakes and never gave herself a moment of comfort or kindness, her unhappiness made her sacrifice worthwhile. And I'd been about to do the same to Poppy.

But if Poppy wanted me not to fight.

Then I wasn't fighting.

I MADE MY way across the back lawn, wondering if Bryant would have wised up since the last time I broke into his house, but no security came to greet me. No bullets stopped me.

I grabbed another apple from the kitchen, didn't bother hiding from the maid who dropped her little dust mop when she saw me. Bryant was already in his study, behind his desk.

He smiled when he saw me and I tossed the thumb drive onto the desk.

"What's this?" he asked.

"Everything the senator did for you."

"The idiot kept it on a thumb drive?"

"Insurance, I imagine. We're done."

"Done?" Bryant got to his feet.

"You got what you paid for. We're done."

"You're turning down my job offer?"

"Aye."

"Is this a fucking joke?"

"No. Not a joke. We have copies of everything on that thumb drive. Come after us and we'll release the information to the FBI and every journalist in New York City."

"Are you threatening me? How very Morelli of you."

I turned and walked away from my uncle. Which predictably, he didn't like.

"That bitch you married—"

I turned on my heel, aware that he was trying to provoke me and I didn't care. I took two steps around the desk before he could shout for one of his bodyguards. I punched him across the face and the old man folded like paper back into his chair.

"That's for touching Poppy. If you threaten her, call her juvenile names, if you so much as look at her again, I will break every bone in your body, Bryant. Do you understand me?

Bryant wiped the smear of blood off his lip. "You could have been so much more, Ronan. So much more than this."

"I'll take what I have," I said. A good woman. Fine friends. A chance at happiness.

And I left Bryant Morelli, like every other person in my life who would use me as a weapon, behind.

I made a quick stop at Poppy's old house to pick up the box that was still on the bed and remembered that Bryant had said he had a box of my mother's. It would have been nice to have those things. Maybe someday I'd break back into his house and get Gwen's things, but that day was not today.

At home I found Poppy on the couch, eating something I didn't make her, which I didn't like.

"Hi," she said, licking the tines of her fork. "What have you been doing?"

"I went to Bryant, told him we were none of his concern."

She put the bowl down and got up on her knees on the couch, happiness dawning on her face. "I also told him if he looked at you funny I'd break every bone in his body." I handed her the box and she clutched it to her chest.

"Thank you," she breathed like I'd handed her the keys to a castle.

"Thank you," I said and pulled her up off the couch into my arms. She'd handed me a future I'd never been able to dream of. A life out of a fairy tale.

"We're free," she whispered.

I'd never been free before. Out of the life. I'd never lived a day that I wasn't in service to violence and violent people. A strange sound erupted out of my throat.

Poppy leaned back, looking at me strangely. "Are you…"

"Laughing, lass. I'm laughing."

She stroked my face. "What do we do now?" she whispered.

"I want to get you pregnant," I told her, walking her backwards to the bedroom.

"Okay, but we need to think outside the bedroom."

"I want a boat."

"For birds and shit?"

"What's wrong with that? I'm a simple man, Poppy. I want to get you pregnant and I want a boat." She blinked at me startled and then her face fell open with a radiant smile. And I swear to God I saw her soul beaming up at me.

"All right, Ronan. Let's get you a boat."

"What do you want?" I asked her and I imagined some answer about taking our money and starting her own foundation to help families. Or maybe going back to school to be a teacher. Or rescuing cats. Some big-hearted soft thing. And I would support her in any of it. All of it. I would take my blood-soaked hands and build gardens all across Northern Ireland if that was what she wanted.

"I just want you," she said and kissed me. I walked her out of that room into the bedroom, where I got on my knees and worshiped her, our future and that little pink bow.

✧   ✧   ✧

Ronan

I LEFT HER sleeping, sated and twitching in her dreams, holding my heart in her cupped palm. How was this going to work, I wondered. Her with all her hope and her feelings. Me with my fallow garden of a soul.

It had to, I thought. Whatever I needed to do to keep her, I would.

She was mine and I was hers. We were married. *With my body I thee worship.*

The words had been said, the promises made. There was no going back. Beneath us, in the rest of the brownstone, I had the sense of my men. Of Niamh. I felt protected, which meant Poppy was protected, and if I woke up every day for the rest of my life and only felt this—it would be enough. But that girl, she would not be content if I wasn't feeling everything. It wouldn't be easy, but I would try. For her.

I made coffee and walked into the living

room.

The jewels had been picked up and put back in the plastic bag. I wondered if Poppy wanted those kinds of things.

Diamonds and the like.

I remembered her, in her life before. There'd been the gala after the senator died and she wore those black pearls like a collar around her neck. I remembered thinking how delicate they made her throat look.

How lovely.

The first thing I was going to do was get rid of that Morelli ring on her finger. It was big and she kept hitting me with it as she slept. It packed a fucking punch.

There was a quiet knock on the door and I went to open it. Raj stood there with a big cardboard box in his hands.

"This came for you, boss," he said and handed it over. On top of the box was a cream envelope sealed with wax. It had the imprint of the Morelli family crest.

I thanked Raj and took the box into the living room and set it down on the table in front of the couch.

I understand these belonged to your mother, so now they belong to you, the letter said. The job offer still stands

Signed Leo Morelli.

It was weird that my hand trembled as I pulled open the box.

Whatever I'd been expecting, little-girl diaries and high school scrapbooks and the like, that wasn't what was in there. There was art. Tons of it. Faded pencil drawings of cats and brighter drawings of flowers and people. One, a woman with dark hair and sad eyes was just marked Eve. Bryant was immortalized in another; she captured his smug upturned nose perfectly.

There were hands, lots of hands, and I had to think they were hers. I held my own up to compare them and then felt foolish. She did a series of watercolors of a black dog at a beach and she captured the dog's joy and the sparkling water so perfectly it felt real. She'd been so talented.

Compelled, I pulled from the wall the picture of the woman I didn't know on a sand dune I'd never been to. There was paper on the back and I tore it off and then carefully pulled the photograph from the glass and replaced it with one of the dogs. I did it with two other pictures. They didn't fit perfectly in the frames, but I liked that about them, too. That I could see the edges of the paper where she'd torn it from the notebook. The smudge of her thumbprint at the bottom corner. It framed the art and its maker.

I took down the rest of the stranger's pictures and found Poppy's framed photographs—the ones Zilla brought when she brought Poppy's jewelry, salvaging the only things Poppy might need from that house. They were sweet photographs of two girls in matching bikinis, their little-girl bellies poking out. I recognized Poppy from her smile. The light that bounced off her. There was another one of Poppy when she was older, high school maybe, with some very unfortunate hair. It was Christmas and she wore a red velvet dress and Zilla wore a sneer and black satin and they stood, hugging a glamorous woman with a distant expression. Their mother. I hung up the photographs on the wall with my mother's art. It didn't make much sense. The sizes of the frames were out of balance, but it was better. It was ours.

Us. I cleared my throat and sat back down. The only thing left in the box was a tin lunch box with an old-school Betty Boop on it. When I opened it a waft of skunky weed floated out from the three joints and Ziplock bag of ancient marijuana in the bottom. Beneath the joints, there was a thin strip of pictures that you get from a photo booth. Four pictures in a row of a young girl with long dark hair. My mom. In the first picture she stared out at the camera, her eyes glittering, her mouth curved into a smile.

She had the look of a person who knew herself.

And who wasn't scared.

There was a guy sitting next to her, with blond floppy hair. Gwen was looking at the camera, he was looking at her like she was his whole world. Loving a Morelli had cost him his life. The second picture he was holding out what looked like a ring box. The third she was crying, her hands over her mouth and the fourth they were kissing. A proposal. She looked so happy.

I flipped over the back of the picture and it said *Me and Danny*. The date was a year and a half almost to the day before I was born. This kid proposed to her, she said yes, her father killed the poor guy and she ran away to England.

Where her whole life ended. Fuck. It was just so sad.

I set aside the picture only to find in the corner of the lunchbox a small faded red velvet ring box.

Impossible, I thought, but opened it anyway. And there on the velvet was a round diamond twinkling madly in the sunlight. It was small. A young man's ring. Bought with a young man's money. But it was a ring that should be worn. Too beautiful to be put away in a box with old memories.

"Hey," Poppy said, walking, sleepy-eyed and wearing one of my tee shirts, into the living room. She yawned with her whole face, a hand over her mouth. "Sorry." She shook her head. I could watch her wake up for years. "What are you doing?"

"Leo sent a box of my mother's things."

She sat down next to me on the couch, her bare legs practically in my lap. As if it was her own, she leaned over and picked up my coffee cup for a sip. "Is this her art?" she asked, picking up a drawing of a cat sleeping on a windowsill. "Oh, Ronan, it's so sweet."

I pointed at the pictures I'd framed, the dog on the beach. And her own pictures of her and her sister and mom hanging beside them. "It's beautiful," she whispered.

"I found this, too." I held out the ring, which caught the sunlight and threw rainbows around the room. It was as if Poppy had been created in ring form. I told her the story of poor Danny.

"And it's been in a box all this time?" she

asked.

I unwrapped her fingers from my coffee mug and slipped the ugly piece of Morelli history off her body. "I'll get you something else later," I told her. "Something you pick out or whatever. But for now it would mean a lot to me if you wore this ring." I slipped the diamond on her finger like it had been made for her.

"It's perfect," she whispered, and kissed me before resting her head on my shoulder. She held it out on her hand, admiring the way it sparkled in sunlight. "I guess it's real, then," she said.

"Us?"

She nodded.

"We're already married."

"You know what I mean." I pulled her up into my lap, sliding my hand over her stomach where there might or might not be a baby we'd made. If wanting her to be pregnant made it so, then she was surely pregnant. If not now, then soon.

"I love you."

"How do you know?" she asked me, stroking my face. Smiling at me because she knew the answer.

Trust. Faith. Surrender. This glowing fucking hope in my chest.

"Because I know."

EPILOGUE

Poppy

THE BLUE OF the sky was the same blue as the sea. It was endless. And you'd think it would get boring, nothing but sea and sky and sun.

But it had been a month, and so far...not boring.

Not boring at all.

Of course, I was very busy.

"Ronan?" I yelled from my spot on the deck. I had cushions and towels and an array of drinks and all the watermelon I could keep down.

"Yeah?"

I turned to find him on the upper deck, the open-air captain's chair. He had his leg propped up on the railing, the damn sketchbook open on his lap.

"Honestly," I said, crossing my arms over my breasts. "It's getting a little pervy, Ronan."

"You're gorgeous," he said. He set down the sketchbook and took the ladder down to the deck where I was lying. He was all sleek tanned muscles in a black swimsuit. His hair was long. He'd lost some of that edge. The lethal grace. He slept through the night, and when the nightmares came for him, I was there to push them away.

To remind him that he was a different man. "And you love it."

He sprawled against my cushions with me. His hands stroking my breasts. The mound of my stomach.

"Lass," he breathed. "You're more beautiful every day."

I stretched my arms over my head. I was tanned from all the sun. Brown all over from sunbathing topless. I was embarrassed at first. Pale and timid.

Feeling like a whale.

But now I am four months pregnant and loving it.

He stroked my hair back from my face.

It was red again. Pulled back in a ponytail. Stiff and curly from the sea air.

"How's the schoolwork?"

"Good," I said. I was taking social work courses online from NYU. I hoped between the courses and all this money we had, Ronan and I might be able to do some real good for kids. Kids like Ronan.

He kissed me. Kissed me again. And I was drunk on sunshine and peace and love but there were realities we needed to deal with.

"We need to get back to harbor soon," I said.

"You feel all right?" he asked, stroking my stomach. He held his hand just above my hip bone, tapping the taut skin until the baby inside of me kicked.

Hi there, son.

Hi there, Dad.

They did this a million times a day, Ronan and his child.

"I'm good, but we're running out of water-melon."

"Then we'd better get back quickly."

I had terrible morning sickness the first three months and I didn't know if it was being on the water that made it better, or if it faded on its own. It was very different from the first time.

Being pregnant was endlessly fascinating.

The monitor at my hip buzzed as Gwen woke up from her nap. She really was the sweetest child. She woke up singing, babbling to herself.

"Grand. I thought she'd never wake up," Ronan said and swung away from me to go get our two-year-old.

Our boat was palatial, larger than the apartment in Brooklyn. And we'd spent a fortune making it as safe as possible. But there were still problems and risks with a two-year-old on a boat, and as he came to the doorway of the cockpit with Gwen in his arms, her red hair in a wild rooster tail on top of her hair, my heart caught in my throat.

Nothing can happen to them.

Nothing will happen to them.

"Mama," she said, and I opened my arms to her. Ronan set her against my skin and she cuddled close. She smelled like sunscreen and baby powder.

"Did you have a good sleep?" I asked her, kissing her cheek.

She rested her head in her hand and babbled at me. I nodded and smiled, only understanding a third of the words she was saying to me. Something about a dog and a fish and a popsicle.

"Poppy," Ronan said, watching us with his heart in his eyes. "I think it's time to go home."

"Yeah?" I asked, watching him over our daughter's head. "You're done being a ferry boat captain?"

He nodded. I'd been expecting this. And truthfully, ready for it for a while.

"Okay, but where is home?"

We'd left New York and had Gwen in Ireland, where Sinead got to be a grandmother and help us through those sleepless first few months. And then we'd gone to Greece and been floating among the islands for six months.

"Back to New York," he said. "You miss your sister."

Zilla had come to visit us. In Ireland when Gwen was born and then again when we picked her up in Athens and took her to Santorini before I was pregnant again. It had been too long and he was right.

"I do," I said. "And you miss Niamh."

He smiled.

He and Niamh and Gwen had almost daily FaceTime calls. He told me about the son she'd left behind and I hoped that Gwen could be a balm on her soul.

"Aye."

Life in our little cocoon was fun but there was a wider world out there. A wider family and I'd found myself missing not just Zilla. And Haley who I'd gotten to know better. But I missed Niamh. Raj. Even Caroline a little bit, which probably wasn't healthy, but family was family even if they were bad.

And Ronan was a man who needed to be of use.

"I think I'd like to go to work for Leo. He keeps offering me that job."

I nodded, stroked our daughter's hair.

"I thought I didn't care about being a Morelli, but Gwen, the babe in your belly, I want them to know family. Cousins and aunts and uncles. We'll keep them safe from the bad ones and let them be loved by the good ones."

I liked the sound of that. The big family I'd dreamed of.

I held out my hand to him and Ronan curled up on the cushions with me and our daughter. We'd cobbled together a kind of happiness I never thought I'd have. It was dense and deep and never-ending. It was safe and sure.

"All right, then. Let's go home."

Thank you for reading UNTAMED! We hope you loved Ronan and Poppy's raw and deep love story. Leo Morelli already has a book you can read next.

The beast hides a dark secret in his past...

Leo Morelli is known as the Beast of Bishop's Landing for his cruelty. He'll get revenge on the Constantine family and make millions of dollars in the process. Even it means using an old man who dreams up wild inventions.

The beauty will sacrifice everything for her family...

Haley Constantine will do anything to protect her father. Even trade her body for his life. The college student must spend thirty days with the ruthless billionaire. He'll make her earn her freedom in degrading ways, but in the end he needs her to set him free.

You can find SECRET BEAST on Amazon, Barnes & Noble, Apple Books, Kobo and Google Play now.

And Tiernan Morelli has a book coming out…

He arrives all dressed in black. Diamond cufflinks. A watch on his tanned wrist that cost more than we would ever see in a lifetime of work. He carries a single red rose for my mother.

Months later, Tiernan Morelli lays red roses on my mother's grave. That same day, he tells me that he is my new guardian.

I should have known from the very start that he had more in common with the thorns than the rose. Now I know the truth: I'm a pawn in his dangerous game of revenge. I was too young and naive. Now it's too late to save myself from his clutches.

Now I belong to him.

You can find DANGEROUS TEMPTATION on Amazon, Barnes & Noble, Apple Books, Kobo and Google Play now.

The warring Morelli and Constantine families have enough bad blood to fill an ocean, and there are told by your favorite dangerous romance

authors. See what books are available now and sign up to get notified about new releases here…
www.dangerouspress.com

About Midnight Dynasty

The warring Morelli and Constantine families have enough bad blood to fill an ocean, and their stories will be told by your favorite dangerous romance authors.

Meet Winston Constantine, the head of the Constantine family. He's used to people bowing to his will. Money can buy anything. And anyone. Including Ash Elliot, his new maid.

But love can have deadly consequences when it comes from a Constantine. At the stroke of midnight, that choice may be lost for both of them.

You can find STROKE OF MIDNIGHT on Amazon, Barnes & Noble, Apple Books, Kobo and Google Play now.

> "Brilliant storytelling packed with a powerful emotional punch, it's been years since I've been so invested in a book. Erotic romance at its finest!"
>
> – #1 New York Times bestselling author Rachel Van Dyken

"Stroke of Midnight is by far the hottest book I've read in a very long time! Winston Constantine is a dirty talking alpha who makes no apologies for going after what he wants."

– USA Today bestselling author
Jenika Snow

Get intimate with the Morellis in this breathtaking new series...

Leo Morelli is known as the Beast of Bishop's Landing for his cruelty. He'll get revenge on the Constantine family and make millions of dollars in the process. Even it means using an old man who dreams up wild inventions.

You can find SECRET BEAST on Amazon, Barnes & Noble, Apple Books, Kobo and Google Play now.

Haley Constantine will do anything to protect her father. Even trade her body for his life. The college student must spend thirty days with the ruthless billionaire. He'll make her earn her freedom in degrading ways, but in the end he needs her to set him free.

These series are now available for you to read!

There are even more books and authors coming in the Midnight Dynasty world, so get started now…

SIGN UP FOR THE NEWSLETTER
www.dangerouspress.com

JOIN THE FACEBOOK GROUP HERE
www.dangerouspress.com/facebook

FOLLOW US ON INSTAGRAM
www.instagram.com/dangerouspress

About the Author

Molly O'Keefe has always known she wanted to be a writer (except when she wanted to be a florist or a chef and the brief period of time when she considered being a cowgirl). And once she got her hands on some romances, she knew exactly what she wanted to write.

She published her first Harlequin romance at age 25 and hasn't looked back. She loves exploring every character's road towards happily ever after.

Originally from a small town outside of Chicago, she went to university in St. Louis where she met and fell in love with the editor of her school newspaper. They followed each other around the world for several years and finally got married and settled down in Toronto, Ontario. They welcomed their son into their family in 2006, and their daughter in 2008. When she's not at the park or cleaning up the toy room, Molly is working hard on her next novel, trying to exercise, stalking Tina Fey on the internet and dreaming of the day she can finish a cup of coffee without interruption.

NEWSLETTER

www.molly-okeefe.com

FACEBOOK

facebook.com/MollyOKeefeBooks

INSTAGRAM

instagram.com/mokeefeauthor

Copyright

Untamed © 2021 by M. O'Keefe
Print Edition

Cover design: Book Beautiful

Printed in Great Britain
by Amazon